e kept

HAMMER
ON THE SEA

HAMMER
ON THE SEA

THEODORE VRETTOS

Little, Brown and Company
Boston · Toronto

LL #3

Published simultaneously in Canada
by Little, Brown & Company (Canada) Limited

PRINTED IN THE UNITED STATES OF AMERICA

For Vas

HAMMER
ON THE SEA

ONE

November opened its eye.

A light snow had fallen during the night, cloaking the mountain with a thin veil of white. Unable to sleep, Stavro left the warmth of the cave to walk into the gorge. He could not chain his mind — he thought about the falling snow, how it was attempting to cover everything — the war, the occupation, famine, death. He felt a sudden urge to scoop up a handful of snow, make a hard ball of it, thrust it in front of God's face and say: *"This is man, a cold ball of snow!"* and then fling it, out into the vast whiteness and again defy God: *"Where is he now, this man You have created? You have swallowed him . . . he does not exist any longer!"*

Strangely, whenever it snowed Stavro thought of Athens . . . it was a day not unlike today — the first snow fell on the city like a young cloud that had strayed from the sky. Stavro had just left the University, in fact had crossed Constitution Square and was about to step into a bus, when he felt that first pang of loneliness. He did not take the bus. Instead he walked, not knowing where he was going, moving rapidly into the white night, past narrow little roads gutted with crippled houses. In his heart he still felt the agony of Socrates' death.

3

After an hour, he came to a shattered door and knocked. Hollow, sunken eyes answered. A thin hand reached out for his. Stavro asked the wrinkled face to point the way back to the University. He explained he was lost. But the old man asked him inside and said: *"You are wet and cold, my son . . . I have no fire to warm you — no food. I can offer you only a glass of water . . . "* They sat in the cold kitchen, both of them sipping from their glasses, talking far into the night. Twice the old man went to his spotless sink to fill the glasses. He was tall, sickly thin, and breathed with his mouth wide open. Yet he walked straight, without shame. His eyes sparkled when Stavro told him he was studying philosophy at the University. *"Why?"* he said to Stavro. *"Why do you want to be a philosopher . . . Are you seeking something?"* Stavro did not have a chance to answer. The withered old man touched him on the shoulder and said, *"Life is not a distant planet waiting to be discovered. It is a heartbeat, so faint and inaudible, you must stop breathing to hear it. You will not find it in the stars, nor in stuffy classrooms . . ."* *"You do not understand,"* Stavro started to say. But the old man plowed on, not listening to him, *"Do you believe in God? I do not mean the goatbeards' God . . . Kyrie eleisons and fastings . . . not that God."* Stavro could not answer him. The old man struggled to his feet. *"I see a great sickness in your eyes,"* he said to Stavro. *"From the moment you walked into my house you have not smiled . . . Is it because you hate God?"* Stavro too got up. He walked to the door, then stopped. *"If I could see God,"* he said, *"I would love Him. . . ."* He opened the door and looked out — the snow had turned to rain. The air felt warm. Before he could take another step the old man's voice bounced back at him: *"You see Him enough to hate Him!"*

It was this same voice Stavro could hear now in the gorge. Despite the howling wind he could clearly make out every word: *"You see Him enough to hate Him!"*

He fought his way back into the cave. Kapetan Thanasi was stretching his arms high, yawning. The others were awake also. Quietly they washed their faces, then huddled around the fire waiting for the coffee to boil. From the time he awoke Stavro was tormented by a strange taste in his mouth. Last night they had all gone to Platano. Kapetan Thanasi insisted — communion before each mission. After church Pappa Lambro invited them to his house. It was a scanty meal: dark bread, olives, a few slices of white cheese.

He met Anna there.

Anna of Athens, nineteen, without family or home . . . light-haired like a Macedonian, she had come to Athens from Crete while still a baby. She spoke of it as though it happened only yesterday: her father returning home from the olive groves at dusk, exhausted . . . sick of nursing a handful of trees year after year . . . nothing to show for his labor but a sunken chest and hacking cough. A new life in Athens! And then the war . . . both her brothers killed in Albania . . . her mother and father unable to survive that first winter of occupation . . . Anna, the last seed of a transplanted Cretan heritage, here now in Platano, living with her father's brother — a priest. Stavro could see her brown eyes catch fire as she spoke. She was like a young mountain goat confined in a cellar — a girl who could not wait to kick off her shoes, toss back her golden hair and start dancing. Anna!

It was Christ who was still warm on Stavro's lips . . . Christ of last night's Eucharist. But now, standing here beside the flames, in this cramped and smelly cave, eight men at his elbows, and rifles propped up in three perfect pyramids, Stavro could feel this same Eucharist burning his mouth. In a few short hours Christ had undergone a second change. He was no longer the Dreamer, the Miracle-Worker . . . the God. Nailed to the cross once again, stretched wide against the narrow wood, His faith wrung dry, Christ had suddenly grown old. Dead.

5

A spoonful of God is not enough.

The coffee was ready. Stavro poured some into his tin and stirred it slowly. His eyes fell on Kleanthi, not yet seventeen; restless thoughts betraying themselves around a boy's tight mouth, bone-white fidgety hands. On Stavro's right hand squatted Panago. Powerful Panago, sitting there, measuring every breath Stavro took, not saying a word.

"Stavro, when are you going to ask Kapetan Thanasi about me?" said Kleanthi, moving in closer to the fire.

"Be patient — your time will come."

"But Pythagora goes on every mission . . ."

Panago sneered, "The little mouse calls it a mission — cutting a few wires at Potami!"

"He was not speaking to you," said Stavro.

"Book-eater, watch your tongue!" Panago folded his hairy arms and waited for Stavro to make a move. Just then, Kapetan Thanasi cradled his mandolin and started playing. His booming voice bounced against the walls of the cave:

> *Old Yero Demos is dying, boys . . .*
> *fifty years a klepht,*
> *and now he is dying . . .*
> *poor Yero Demos!*

They finished their coffee. The four men chosen for Potami warmed their hands for the last time before going into their bandoliers. Stavro picked up his rifle. Panago, still fuming, grabbed the wire cutters. Pythagora was the first to leave the cave. Kleanthi stood sad-eyed by the fire, fighting to hold back the tears. Stavro touched him on the shoulder. "Kleanthi, remember — if there is any trouble here, two shots into the air and we will come quickly."

When Stavro entered the gorge and saw how the new snow had taken the great pillars of stone and transformed them into immaculate statues, he stopped for a moment, certain that something had touched the veins of his guilt — that

6

same haunting echo he had heard many times before, cutting through the harsh wind, bouncing off the white temples, flooding his ears: *"Stavro, what are you doing with that gun in your hands? Go back . . . go back!"*

2

Potami was five twisting miles up a perilous mountain pass. It slept between two towering peaks in the northernmost slope of Mount Taugetos. The plan, however, called for the wires to be cut not in the village but at a point three miles north. After bypassing Potami they came to the place at noon, just when the clouds thinned out and the sun came streaking down. It was desolate and surrounded by sharp cliffs through which passed, hand-in-hand, a narrow goat path and swollen stream. Kapetan Thanasi sent Pythagora to a steep ledge that commanded a clear view of the path from both ends. Panago wanted to go down for a drink of water but Kapetan Thanasi would not allow it.

They waited.

Three men concealed in snow and rock, the vicious wind biting at their fingers and toes. Twice, Kapetan Thanasi got up to check on Pythagora. The minutes lost themselves . . . minutes bursting into a million thoughts . . . a million hands taking hold of Stavro's mind, pulling it back . . . back to the day his youngest brother, Stellio, died. But he should not think about that now.

An old goatherd came trudging down the path with half a dozen scrawny goats lagging behind him. When the goats saw the stream they made a run for it, but the old man was impatient and made them move on.

Again they waited.

Life was one long wait for Stavro. He had waited for the Italians, and now the Germans who leave only a dead donkey for a boy of fourteen to eat . . . but he was not going to think about Stellio.

For the third time Kapetan Thanasi left them. Stavro followed him out. Panago remained in the rocks, clutching his rifle — his mind only on that. They heard a muffled cry from the ledge. Pythagora was running toward them, waving both hands and crying, "Cycles, Kapetan — three of them!"

"Are you certain they are not goats?" Panago smirked. He too had left the rocks and was suddenly standing beside them.

"What shall we do, Kapetan?" said Pythagora, panting.

"Let them pass," said Kapetan Thanasi.

"No . . . kill them!" cried Panago. The loud whirr of motors echoed against the rocks, drowning his voice. Three cycles came into view. Stavro heard Panago muttering under his breath, "Come closer, my white-haired ducks . . . closer . . ."

Again Pythagora tossed an anxious look at Kapetan Thanasi. "Let them pass," said the Kapetan, his eyes never leaving the cycles.

"No!" bellowed Panago in a barbaric voice.

"Look, they are stopping," said Pythagora.

Kapetan Thanasi turned to say something to Stavro. Cursing loudly, Panago took aim with his rifle and fired. One of the cyclists fell to the ground. The other two leaped from their cycles and ran for the rocks. Panago fired again but missed. He fired once more — the Germans disappeared behind the rocks.

All four slid down the cliff after them. When they reached the path Stavro stopped and edged his way toward the fallen German. The others lost themselves behind the rocks. Stavro's heart pounded hard as he watched the last convulsions. He could not pull his eyes away from the blood pouring out of the German boy's mouth and flowing wantonly on the thin crust of frozen snow. A flurry of rifle shots. Cries of *"Aera . . . Aera!"* Death and joy in the same breath.

Stavro remained by the German boy. He waited. He gave life ample time to revert to death and when he was confident he had won, he saw the boy's hand move. Stavro brought up his rifle slowly, no higher than his waist. He still hoped he would not have to use it. But the bronze face tormented him. The straining eyes twisted with pain, inviting him, begging him to fire.

"Shoot!" a thunderous voice fell on his back. He turned, saw Panago bring up his rifle and pump two quick shots into the German boy's head that made sounds like drops of water on a hot stove . . . Waves of nausea engulfed Stavro. He saw the others coming out of the rocks. Weakly, he pulled out a cigarette and lit it. Kapetan Thanasi was walking slowly, dragging his rifle along the snow. Without looking at Stavro, he said, "Is this one dead?"

"Yes," said Stavro, aware that Panago was challenging him with a contemptuous look. Pythagora pushed himself between them. He could not wait to say it: "Stavro, we got the Germans . . . both of them!" He had an odd grin on his face, that of a boy who had just smoked his first cigarette.

"Did you remember to bring the brandy?" Kapetan Thanasi asked him.

"Yes," said Pythagora. He clamped both knees together as though he had to urinate and was trying to hold it back. Kapetan Thanasi and Panago took long drinks from the bottle. Pythagora then went to hand it to Stavro but he pushed it away. Staring proudly at his hands, Panago sauntered over to where the German boy lay. He stooped over him for a long while, staying there until Kapetan Thanasi called out to him, "The wires, Panago!"

Panago straightened up and walked toward the nearest pole. After he had climbed to the top he gave two quick snips with the cutters; the dead wires slithered to the ground.

"We had better move out," said Kapetan Thanasi. His voice sounded very tired. Pythagora noticed the rifle lying beside the dead German boy and went after it.

"Leave it!" Stavro yelled. Pythagora looked up, stunned. Again he reached down for the rifle.

"I said . . . *leave it!*"

9

Bewildered, Pythagora kept shifting his eyes from the rifle to Stavro. Slowly, he walked away from it. They moved out in one line, Kapetan Thanasi leading the way. When they reached the top of the slope overlooking Potami, Stavro discovered the wind had suddenly veered. Gentle Zephyr pushed merciful gusts over the mountain, warming their frozen fingers and toes. Stavro dropped back to the end of the line beside Pythagora. The boy had his eyes fastened on the snow, trying desperately to walk on the prints Panago was leaving behind.

"Where is the brandy?" Stavro asked him.

Fumbling with his sack, Pythagora unhooked a pocket and pulled out the bottle. There was very little brandy left in it. Stavro bit away the cork and drank. Clamping his knees together again, Pythagora said, "What has come over you, Stavro?"

Stavro tossed the bottle into the snow. Quickly Pythagora ran to retrieve it. He wiped it clean with the palms of his hands and tucked it carefully into the pocket of his sack.

They walked on, neither of them speaking for a long time.

"Stavro, why did you not want me to take the rifle?" Pythagora finally said.

Stavro did not answer. Forcing his knees together once more, Pythagora said, "Stavro, when we ran into the rocks one of the Germans saw us and tried to get away. Panago said to me: 'Look, Pythagora — your first German!' I missed him but Panago waited for me to shoot again. Three times, Stavro . . . three times . . ."

They entered the gorge.

A heavy melancholy filled Stavro's heart when he saw how the sun had melted the glistening temple of white statues and turned everything into muted stone again. Kleanthi saw them from the cave and came running. Pythagora hurried to meet him. "Aera! Aera!" he shouted, and they fell into each other's arms.

10

3

He went to his mother's house early the next day with a chicken and a bottle of olive oil. For the first time in several weeks he slept well. In the morning he awoke with the church bell. As he dressed he felt a hungry desire to look into Anna's face.

His mother was in the kitchen making coffee. She had her black shawl thrown over her shoulders. He was certain she heard him but she did not turn around.

"The coffee will be ready soon," she said in a hollow voice. Her brown hair was still uncombed, her face not washed. He walked to the door, opened it, and stepped outside. It was still dark. The earth and sky were stuck together in one gray shadow. A strong scent was coming from the sea, and in the distance, cutting sharply toward the mountains, Stavro could make out a thin necklace of gulls, white bodies flashing against the dense sky, muffled cries filling the air with vain protests against an awakening world. He remembered something: the look on his mother's face when he first told her he was going to Athens. His father was alive then — sitting here in this same kitchen, not saying a word in his defense.

"You are bringing a chill into the house," he heard his mother say. And quickly she added, "The coffee is ready."

After breakfast he put on his sweater and jacket. His mother came with him as far as the porch. "Stavro," she said, "please be careful . . ."

"Cook the chicken," he told her. "I will be back for supper." She turned and walked slowly into the house. As he swung across the yard toward the groves, he felt a heavy pounding in his head. It always came to this: lying awake in the cave at night, worrying about her, wondering if she had enough to eat, hoping she was not ill. And always that suffering look in her eyes whenever he came down from the mountain . . . her scar of loneliness torn open once again, filling his soul with guilt.

On his left hand, his father's olive trees looked deprived, unwanted — like an old man sick and about to die. The thought numbed Stavro: this was his father's land, every inch of earth and sky. Stavro had breathed his life here . . . yes, and he had died his father's death here, many times over — his mother would never let him forget that!

He reached the square and quay in time to see the sun stretching his fingers over the Aegean. Already the mist enshrouding Taugetos had lifted, baring the mountain's wide flanks and snow-covered peaks.

Perched on a wooden crate just at the entrance to the quay, old Pelopida, his brown cane resting across his bony thighs, peered angrily at the empty harbor. Pelopida, the bull, producer of eight sons and two daughters, gripping his cane and glaring at the water — seeing perhaps Charon, the Ferryman and Transporter of the Dead. When he heard Stavro he narrowed his eyes at him and said, "Ah, the philosopher! What brings you here so early . . . have you come to light a candle along with these other fools?"

Stavro tried to sit beside him but Pelopida would not make room for him. He had ample space on both sides of the crate, yet he refused to move. When the church bell started in again the old man winced with pain. He made faces. Pointing his cane menacingly at Saint John's blue dome, he cried out, "Hey John, shut your mouth . . . God is a deaf-mute, you fool. He cannot hear you . . . your *Kyrie eleisons* are a hammer on the sea!"

Shifting himself more securely on the crate now, he said to Stavro, "How is that worthless son of mine?"

A caïque rounded the breakwater and drifted into the harbor. Stavro followed it all the way to the quay before speaking. "I asked Kleanthi to come down with me," he said, "but he did not want to."

12

"The devil take him!"

"He said he would be down for Christmas. . . ."

Staring more defiantly at the sea, Pelopida roared, "Christmas, is that what he said? Will I be here myself for Christmas?" The bell finally stopped. A solitary gull came soaring back from the mountains and lighted on the water beside the caïque. Stavro turned to walk away.

"Wait, what is your hurry?" yelled Pelopida. He slid quickly off the crate and came scrambling after Stavro. They walked into the square together. Several small children were playing beneath the great plane tree — chasing each other happily, filling the air with innocence. Three girls and a boy. One of the little girls recognized Stavro and dashed into his arms. He swung her high above his head, holding her there as she screamed with joy. She was bones, skin, and brown hair. She felt no heavier than a bag of chicken feathers. For a fleeting instant he looked into her large eyes and saw Greece there — starving, dying . . . a bag of chicken feathers! Now she began squirming and struggling to free herself. Stavro kissed her on the cheek before letting her go. He glanced back and saw Pelopida, both hands on his cane, fascinated by the little girl's bare legs. Disgustedly, Stavro walked away from him. He heard the old man calling him but he kept walking.

A cluster of women stood near the steps of the church jabbering into each other's faces. Stavro saw the huge oak door opening — Pappa Lambro came out. His beard looked wild; the right elbow of his robe was worn through, food stains were caked along the front of it. He seemed very haggard and thin. Stavro rushed to meet him. Taken by surprise, Pappa Lambro offered him his hand. Stavro shook it — he did not kiss it. From the day Stellio died he vowed he would never kiss a priest's hand again.

"Stavro," cried Pappa Lambro, "you are with us again?"

"Yes."

"Did everything go well yesterday at Potami?"

"Yes."

"No one was hurt?"

"No one."

Pappa Lambro crossed himself. They walked into the priest's yard together. His wife was bent over her basil pots, covering them with sheets of white cloth. "Where is Anna?" said Stavro.

The priest's wife gave him a stern look, then said, "Still in bed."

"She is not ill?"

Pappa Lambro let out a loud laugh. "The Cretans do not have our schedule, Stavro — I am afraid Anna is still sleeping." He led Stavro into the kitchen after first making a sign to his wife. She stepped into the pantry and brought out a small jar of sugared lemon peel. Spooning it out into two plates, she placed them on a tray, together with two glasses of water, and brought them to the table. Pappa Lambro's face suddenly grew austere. He did not touch the sweets. Meanwhile Stavro, his heart racing, threw an anxious look toward the stairs, hoping to catch Anna's first footsteps. After a long silence he said to the priest, "Why was the bell ringing this morning?"

Pappa Lambro looked up at him, surprised. "Stavro," he said, "the bell rings every day . . . matins, vespers, special canons to the Virgin . . . only God can save us now!"

His wife excused herself and returned to her basil pots. The pain in Pappa Lambro's eyes seemed to grow more intense. "Stavro," he said, "every moment of the day I beg God to spare Platano — to spread His arms over us and keep us from harm. When I think of what happened to Arka. . . ."

For months now, Stavro had forced himself to forget Arka . . . its few dozen white houses glued to a lazy slope, half of it climbing toward Taugetos, the other half dropping quietly down to the sea . . . the narrow little quay, the immaculate church glistening in the sun, endless groves of cypresses stretching their slender bird-filled arms into the sky . . . the long swim across the bay with ribs of dynamite sticks laced around his head . . . eruption . . . death! And then the quick reprisal: the immaculate church burned to the ground, the white houses charred forever, the cypresses drooped in morning, the birds gone. . . .

" . . . my soul bleeds, Stavro . . . it bleeds!"

There was a sound of new footsteps on the porch. The kitchen door swung open; Pelopida came limping in. He brandished his cane at Stavro and croaked, "Why did you not wait for me?" But before Stavro could answer, Pelopida snapped at the priest, "Do you have any wine?"

Pappa Lambro went to the pantry and brought out a bottle. He poured a glass for Pelopida as the old man's eyes skirted around the room. Taking the glass, he said, "Where is the Cretan?"

"She is upstairs," said Pappa Lambro.

Pelopida took a loud sip, then wiped his lips with the back of his hand. "Have you two fixed the day?" he said. When he got no reply the old man slammed his glass on the table and roared, "Are we going to have a wedding or are we not?"

Pappa Lambro quieted him by pouring more wine into his glass. Pelopida downed it quickly; his face brightened. He started to tell them about his oldest son . . . how he died on the Albanian front. As the old man talked, Stavro's own thoughts slid back to Athens. He remembered how brilliantly the sun swarmed over the Acropolis — he had never seen such light before, so breathless and powerfully alive. It was as though he were surrounded by a whole universe of suns, each of them streaking down upon him, saturating him, reaching every inch of his soul until he had lost all identity, all awareness of time. . . .

Pelopida was on something else now . . . when he served in the Red Legion and thousands of Turkish heads fell. At

15

one point the old man lifted his arm and waved it violently, crying, "Long live the Red Legion . . . long live Greece!" Tears flowed out of his eyes. Stavro felt a new compassion for him — he wanted to sweep the old man into his arms, assure him that Greece would crawl out from under the German boot and breathe freely once again. He would have done so if he had not heard more footsteps, the rustle of a swirling skirt, the soft sigh of astonishment escaping from Anna's lips. She came and stood beside him, looking straight into his eyes — unmindful of her uncle, the priest . . . unmindful of Pelopida, gripping his cane and squinting hard at her.

Feeling the world's eyes upon him, Stavro pushed back his chair and clumsily got to his feet.

"Anna," he said.

4

He went to visit his Uncle Petro and Aunt Zacharo later that afternoon with his mother. Charon's finger had touched Zacharo — Zacharo, who once could carry three live goats on her back and dig out great boulders from the fields as if they were tiny pebbles, slouched here now on the sofa, her face waxen, her body wasting away, her mind contemplating the end of all things . . . ignoring Stavro's playful fingers on her bony cheek.

His mother left them to go into the kitchen. She came back with four small plates of grape preserve, carrying them on a battered copper tray. Stavro put his aside. Before anyone could speak, the front door opened and Pappa Lambro walked in. From his coat pocket he pulled out a bottle and handed it to Petro — it was red wine. Overwhelmed, Petro crossed himself. "Why are you doing this, Pappa?" he said. "What can I possibly give you in return? I had a hillful of goats once . . . also two strong sons and, begging your pardon, one daughter . . . I had all these things, Pappa. . . ." He stopped to wipe his eyes.

Pappa Lambro cleared his throat and said, "I was in Potami yesterday."

"So?" said Petro.

"I go there occasionally to visit with old Pappa Thoma. We exchange a little oil for wine . . . he told me the Germans had been there. He said. . . ."

"We have nothing to do with Potami," Petro interrupted him. As if coming out of a trance, Zacharo perked up her face and mumbled, "We have done nothing wrong . . . nothing wrong."

Pappa Lambro was about to go on when a loud knock on the door stopped him. It was Pelopida. "I was sitting by the window in the coffeehouse," he explained to Petro, "when I saw the priest climbing your steps. Has it happened . . . I mean, Zacharo?"

"Do you not see her on the sofa?" Petro retorted.

"She still lives?"

"She lives and reigns!" cried Pappa Lambro, forcing a smile for everyone's benefit. Red-faced, Pelopida walked to the sofa and put his hand on Zacharo's head. He did not speak. His knees cracked loudly as he sat down beside her. Petro went into the kitchen for more glasses. He poured one for Pelopida first, then the others. The old man kept glaring at the priest.

"What have you done about the cobbler's son, Pappa?" he shouted.

Pappa Lambro scowled. "Forget the cobbler's son."

"You promised me . . . I was the first to ask!"

"It is too late."

"You buried him . . . you buried him with his clothes on?" Pelopida exclaimed. He struggled to get up but the priest pushed him back down again.

17

"It was the mother's wish," said Pappa Lambro with an emphatic sigh.

"The shoes . . . how about the shoes?" said Pelopida.

"He is wearing those also."

Pelopida grunted out loud; he spat at the ceiling. Petro leaned over to fill the old man's glass. Stavro caught the twisted grin forming on his uncle's mouth. "Pelopida," Petro said, "there is still time. Let Pappa Lambro here say the word; we will go to the cemetery and dig the boy out. You can have whatever you wish . . . shoes, pants, shirt, tie. . . ."

Pelopida jabbed the point of his cane into the floor, enraged. "Do you take me for a ghoul?" he cried. With this, Pappa Lambro suddenly stiffened. He smoothed down his beard and in the voice of a high priest declared, "Petro, the dead sleep in sacred ground. It is a sin to even think such thoughts!"

It was the manner in which he said it that bothered Stavro — the infallible voice of the ages, Lazarus resurrected, returned to the world of the living . . . Lazarus bearing witness to the agony, the gnashing of teeth, the fearful spectacle of death.

"Are you certain about the shoes?" Pelopida asked once more.

"Was I not there?" yelled Pappa Lambro in that same voice. "Did I not see the boy with my own eyes?"

Zacharo moaned weakly and slumped back on the sofa. Stavro's mother helped her upstairs. After they were gone Pappa Lambro said to Petro, "Zacharo looks better today."

Petro gave him a sour look. "You say the same thing every time you come here, Pappa."

"Once the glass is cracked, it can never be repaired," Pelopida announced. Stavro could bear to hear no more. He got up and walked to the front window. The square looked deserted. A gull stood perched on the gold cross of the church, staring at the mountains. It fluttered its wings and began screeching loudly as if to warn Platano a third severe winter lurked on the other side of Taugetos. Already the olive leaves had changed color, the earth tightened its womb, the sea heaved restlessly like a delirious child in the throes of a fever.

"Where is the Cretan?" Pelopida asked the priest.

"Why do you always ask?" snapped back Pappa Lambro. Pelopida's answer was an angry growl at his empty glass. No one filled it for him. Petro gave a loud slap on his thigh and said to the priest, "Pappa, I have something on my mind."

"Speak."

"I am not pulling your beard, Pappa — but something bothers me about . . . well, about Him."

The priest looked up, perplexed.

"He means God," said Pelopida, still grunting at his empty glass. Stavro finally filled it for him. "Yes," said Petro, "from the time we are small children you goatbeards clamor away at us, trying to prove how wise God is."

"Certainly," said Pappa Lambro, in the voice of the high priest again. "There is nothing that God does not know. Even the hairs on your head are numbered. . . ."

Pelopida let out a disgruntled laugh. Rubbing his bald pate vigorously, he said, "I was a bush once . . . a great thick bush! But look at me now — I have a naked fish on my head. If you ask me, God has more important things to do than count hairs."

The gull on the cross flew off. A heavy cloud of dejection fell on Stavro. *Had he dealt with his soul wrongly? Should he have taken hold of it by the throat as his uncle was doing this very moment, sitting here in the company of an emaciated priest, a withered old man . . . joking, drinking, devouring the hour . . . doing all this while Zacharo was upstairs dying out her life . . . ?*

"Pappa, before I say another word, I want it clearly understood that I speak as a philosopher, not a Greek Orthodox," Petro said. Pelopida laughed at this; Petro got angry. "What is so funny, old man?" he shouted. "Can I not be a philosopher too . . . must I have a degree from Athens? Did Socrates have a degree . . . did Christ?"

"Go on," said Pappa Lambro impatiently.

"Remember what I said, Pappa. . . ."

"Yes, yes — that you speak as a philosopher."

"I do not want you to slam the church door in my face."

"Have no fear," said Pappa Lambro. Petro's face lit up. "This is what I want to ask you, Pappa — did Zeus actually tell Adam and Eve to multiply?"

"Not Zeus. God!" the priest immediately corrected him. "Yes, He told them to be fruitful . . . to multiply and inherit the earth."

Petro smirked. "This was His first mistake. He should have said to them: *'Adam and Eve, you have every good thing here in Paradise . . . eat, drink, and ask no questions. Above all, do not let me catch you with your clothes off.'* "

"They did not wear clothes in those days," said Pelopida with a loud grunt of authority. The priest also assented to this. He said, "Yes, Adam and Eve were in a state of eternal bliss and as such, were totally unaware of their nakedness."

"This is my point precisely, Pappa. Could not Zeus see how wrong it was, putting a naked man and woman together?"

"Why do you persist in calling Him Zeus?" Pappa Lambro cried, getting aggravated. Taking out his handkerchief he wiped the sweat from his face. "Petro," he said, "man's conception of God has changed. The myths of Olympus have vanished into thin air. We have only one God now. . . ."

"Yes, Zeus."

"No, not Zeus. God!"

"I do not understand you, Pappa — what is this other one's name?"

"He has no name. He is just . . . just God!"

2 0

Still wearing that grin, Petro edged his way toward Stavro. "Nephew," he said, "goatbeard here is pinning me down. Give your uncle a philosopher's helping hand."

"Books do not make philosophers," shouted Pelopida.

"Close your mouth," said Petro. "What do you know about philosophy?"

"I know enough to keep quiet."

Turning to the priest, Petro said, "Pappa, I have one final word to say to you — we must stop deluding ourselves. We all know the real reason why Zeus punished Adam and Eve."

Pelopida instantly came erect. As if dreading what Petro would say next, Pappa Lambro began stroking his beard nervously.

"It was not the apple," Petro said.

"Not the apple?" cried Pelopida.

"Certainly not. Put yourselves in Zeus' sandals — would not your blood boil with jealousy if you saw those two enjoying each other before your very eyes?"

"Preposterous!" yelled Pappa Lambro. He left his chair and walked to the front door. Pelopida struck his temple with both hands. "Petro," he moaned, "you have me so confused I do not know what to believe."

Fuming, Pappa Lambro raised his hands to silence him. He looked at Pelopida when he spoke. "Belief in God comes not from the head, but the heart."

His words set Stavro on fire. He leaped before the priest and cried, "No . . . no! It comes from the belly."

"What did you say?" Pappa Lambro asked him, shocked.

"It comes from the belly!" Stavro shouted. "God is where your belly is. . . ."

Very ill at ease now, Pappa Lambro reached for his coat. Petro helped him with it. Contritely he laughed. "Pappa, promise you will not excommunicate me."

The priest brought up his fingers and touched Petro's head.

"God is merciful," he said and opened the door. Before leaving, his eyes touched Stavro for a painful instant.

5

An hour later Petro was asleep on the sofa. Stavro pulled his chair up alongside the window and sat down. His mind was a nest of snakes — he could not understand what came over him. He had never shown such anger before, let alone to Pappa Lambro, whom he had loved since he was a child. The remorse cut deeper into his heart when he heard the vesper bell clang. The square quickly came alive. A line of women, their heads draped with black shawls, moved up the street toward the church. The children surrounded the plane tree once again to resume their play. Very soon, thought Stavro, the church would suffocate from Pappa Lambro's censer . . . his sad incantations would begin, the women's sobs, their tears . . . and after the priest had chanted David's song, and the smoke and prayers had thinned out . . . after everyone had gone home to empty tables and empty hopes, perhaps this shadow of a God might weep for them and show His face.

Hanging limply from the iron railing below the church tower, the Blue and White seemed cramped between her two conquerors. Stavro now realized that his uncle had awakened and was standing beside him. Petro too glared at the flags. *"Christ between the two thieves!"* he snarled. Just then Stavro's mother came downstairs. She tossed her shawl over her back and said to Stavro, "It is getting late."

But Stavro could not release his eyes from the flags. A new wretchedness found his heart. "Why must Aunt Zacharo die?" he said. The words almost choked him. Petro started to say, "Stavro, these things are out of our hands. . . ."

"Your uncle is right," his mother interjected. "We have

22

told you this many times . . . you cannot solve life with questions."

"Stavro, you are twenty-three years old," bellowed Petro. "It is not healthy to think as much as you do — you will make yourself ill. I have wanted to say this to you for a long time — even before you went to Athens to become a philosopher."

"I did not go to Athens for that reason."

". . . and now this guerrilla business . . . living in caves like an animal. This is not for you, Stavro. Can you not see how unhappy you have made your mother?"

"Will it make her happy if I chain myself to her olive trees?"

"Not her trees, Stavro . . . *yours!*"

"Nothing is mine that does not come from these two hands."

"I do not want to fight with you," said Petro.

"He is your uncle," his mother cried. "Listen to him — he speaks for your good."

Petro touched him on the shoulder. "Stavro, I beg you, give up this foolishness. Return to your mother's house . . . stay with her — at least until the Germans leave."

"They will not leave unless we make them."

"Nonsense! Can you not see the harm you are doing? For every German you kill — fifty of us die." Petro was about to say more but he saw Stavro's mother putting on her coat. "No, Marika," he yelled. "Do not leave yet — stay for supper, please."

"Petro, you have hardly enough food for Zacharo."

"Marika, I want you to stay — Pappa Lambro brought some chick peas yesterday, enough for all of us to eat." He pulled away Marika's coat and forced her into the kitchen. Reluctantly she nodded her head. While Stavro sat with his uncle at the table she filled an earthen pot with water and placed it over the jaki to boil. Petro suddenly threw his arm over Stavro and in a booming voice cried, "Nephew, I have just now made up my mind. I want you to take me with you when you go back into the mountains."

Stavro laughed.

"I am serious," Petro exclaimed. "I want you to take me with you. . . ."

Marika heard him and turned sharply about. "No, Petro," she said.

Petro looked into her eyes. "Marika, Stavro is right — the Germans will not leave unless we make them. I must tell you something . . . listen, both of you. What have I done for my country, for my church? When the day comes for Charon to lift me on his shoulders and carry me off, what will I say to him . . . that in all my forty-eight years I never once lifted a finger to help either the Cross or the Blue and White? What shall I say to your father, Stavro — my dead brother, Costa? I know what his first words will be: *'Petro, did you pick up your gun . . . did you fight for Greece?'* If I tell him I sat on my hands throughout the whole war he will spit in my face and never speak to me again. . . ."

"Petro, I know what you are trying to say." Marika left the jaki and drew closer to him. But Petro slammed his fist on the table and snapped back at her, "No, you do not understand! I know what both of you are thinking . . . *This is Petro talking again, Petro, the coward . . . Petro, who shit in his pants when the Italians climbed into Greece. . . .*"

"That is not true," said Marika, giving him a merciful look. "Petro, you were sick."

"I was afraid, Marika — not sick!"

All this time Stavro said nothing. He got up from his chair and walked to the door. He did not open it; he stood there, staring blankly at the knob, fighting with all his strength not to say the ugly thoughts that were pinching his brain. Disgustedly, he went to open the door.

"Stavro, wait!" Petro cried, rushing toward him. His face

was wet with tears. "Stavro, I beseech you — put your ear to my heart . . . you will hear years of misery and shame. Do it, Stavro. Look inside me and see Christ standing there, holding a great sponge in His hand. He is speaking to me, Stavro . . . He is saying: *'Petro, for forty-eight years you have stunk so badly I could not come near you. But today I am proud of you . . . here, let me wash your hands and your feet. . . .'*"

The soft tinkle of a bell outside interrupted him. Petro started for the door. "No!" Stavro warned, pushing him away. He crept to the window and looked out. Two men in gray-green uniforms were standing on the porch — one was an officer, a lieutenant. He was ringing the bell. The soldier with him had his feet planted wide apart and was aiming his rifle at the door.

"Germans!" Petro shouted. He hurled his eyes toward the cellar door, his face white, his whole body trembling . . . Petro, who only a moment ago was washed clean by Christ . . . now frozen in fear, feeling the weight of Christ's finger on his soul, ashamed to lift his head, too mortified to go through still another ablution . . . this same Petro blindly sweeping the cellar door open and fleeing downstairs.

Marika ran to the door. Stavro made a desperate lunge for her — at the same time digging his other hand into his jacket pocket for the revolver . . . the German revolver. But eluding his grasp, Marika threw him a mother's look and flung open the door. Stavro ran back to the window and parted the curtains with the muzzle of the revolver. Every word came back to him clearly:

"Where are the men of this house?" the lieutenant asked Marika in fluent Greek. The soldier beside him pawed her with cold eyes. Stavro heard his mother say, "My husband is dead."

"Where are your sons?"

"I have no sons."

"You are lying!"

25

"Come, see for yourself," Marika said, pointing to the door. "I am alone with my cousin . . . she is in her bed upstairs, dying. . . ."

"Where is her husband?"

"Dead . . . he and his children . . ." Marika broke into sobs. Unmoved, the lieutenant placed his bronze bell on the porch floor and drew out a cigarette from a slender black case. He lit it and inhaled deeply. "Where was your husband killed?" he said.

"Near Koritsa."

A hard grin crept over the lieutenant's face. He drew another deep puff from his cigarette. "And your son, where was he killed?"

"I have no sons!" Marika screamed. She slumped back against the porch railing, reeled, and fell to her knees. The lieutenant did not move to help her. Stooping for his bell, he said, "We do not want to harm you . . . I ask you for the final time — where is your husband?"

"He is dead!"

"Your sons . . . ?"

"I have no sons!"

"Where is your cousin's husband?"

"Dead . . . dead!" Marika moaned. Her cries burned Stavro's ears. He tightened his finger over the trigger and aimed at the lieutenant's heart. He was about to fire when the lieutenant suddenly turned his head around to whisper something to the soldier. Quickly, they both swung away from the porch and hurried out of the yard. As soon as they were gone, Stavro ran to his mother. He lifted her in his arms and carried her inside. She was near hysterics — she clutched him tightly, digging her nails into his back.

He eased her into a chair just as the cellar door opened. Petro crawled out. He had the gaunt look of a man who had spent most of his life in a dungeon. His eyes were blood-red. "Marika," he choked, never withdrawing his shamed

gaze from Stavro, "I beg you for a mother's word to her son
. . . please, Marika, make Stavro take me with him . . .
please!"

6

Later as they sat to eat, Zacharo called out to them from
the top of the stairs, "What is it . . . what did they want?"
When no one answered her she came down and stood weakly beside the table. Marika stopped eating and took hold of
her arm but Zacharo pulled it away. She looked at Stavro
and said, "What did the Germans want . . . tell me!"

Stavro leaned over and pinched her on the cheek. He said
to himself: *This is not my Aunt Zacharo — these jutting
cheekbones and sunken eyes, this yellow skin. . . ."*

"It is nothing," he assured her. "They asked a few questions and left. No one was harmed."

Petro pushed his plate away and buried his head in his
hands. "Take her upstairs," he said to Marika. Stavro got
up before his mother and took his aunt by the hand. He
helped her upstairs. When they reached the bedroom door
he playfully jabbed his fingers into her hard ribs, trying to
get her to giggle as she always used to do when she was well.
Instead, she began weeping. She lifted her suffering eyes to
Stavro. "I want you to take your uncle into the mountains. . . ."

"But, Aunt Zacharo. . . ."

"Do it for me, Stavro — Christ will bless you for it."

He helped her to the bed. Guardedly, he kissed her on the
forehead — it felt like a cold slab of marble. "We can talk
about this some other time," he said. "You must try to get
some sleep now."

Back in the kitchen he saw his uncle staring out the window, his eyes red again. Marika took a bowl of soup up-

stairs for Zacharo. While she was gone Stavro put on his sweater and jacket.

"Where are you going?" Petro asked him. Stavro pushed him away and opened the door. Petro clamped a fierce hand over his shoulder. "Stavro," he said, "do nothing foolish!" Still not speaking to him, Stavro pulled away and closed the door. In the yard a swirling wind struck him in the face, while above him the sky gave birth to millions of stars. To Stavro they seemed like mirages of hope.

A light was on in the priest's house. Anna answered the door — she had been crying. The priest's wife sat rigidly on the lumpy red sofa, wringing her hands and mumbling words that Stavro could not piece together. As though startled from a bad dream, she got up and flung herself into Stavro's arms, wailing, "They took Pappa Lambro . . . the Germans took him, Stavro!"

He made her sit down but could not calm her. Between fitful sobs she told Stavro everything: the tinkling bell, Anna pleading with her uncle not to go to the door . . . Pappa Lambro's last words, *I am a priest of God — they cannot harm me. . . .*"

"Where did they take him?" said Stavro.

"We do not know," Anna blurted out. Stavro started for the door. Before he could open it Anna was in his arms. "Wait, I am coming with you," she said.

"No. I do not want you to leave this house — do you understand?" But she was too terrified to listen to him. He waited for her to stop crying. "Anna," he whispered, "there is nothing to fear. I will find Pappa Lambro — I promise you."

7

He hurried through the square. Fearlessly, the moon showed itself — full-grown like a ripe orange. The dim silhouettes of houses seemed flattened against the black sky and sea, as though they were cut out of paper and pasted there. He reached the northern row of cypresses that guarded the cemetery like giant sentinels. Stopping there for a minute to catch his breath, he then circled around the church to the back steps. He shuddered when he did not find the priest in the altar. He moved quickly past the Holy Table and immediately after he had done so he remembered what Pappa Lambro once told him when he was an altar boy — " . . . *never walk across the Holy Table, for you will cast a shadow on Christ, sleeping here inside the chalice . . ."* Stavro felt a strong urge to cross himself but fought it off. Dimly, he recalled it was at Stellio's funeral he last crossed himself; he vowed then he would never do it again. Three fingers to the temple, the stomach, the shoulders . . . and now the words — say them slowly, with reverence and feeling: *"Thou art Holy, oh God . . . Holy and Strong . . . Holy and Deathless, have mercy upon us . . . !* Again. God will not hear you unless you repeat it three times. The formula . . . everything must be done in triplicate — fingers, words, Kyrie eleisons, Amen . . . then only will the cock crow and God will listen.

The smell of vespers still lay heavy in the church. The holy lights sputtered beneath the icons, thirsting for oil. The school was a long rectangular hall adjacent to the west wall of the church — one door connected both. In the rich moonlight Stavro recognized the desk — the same desk he sat in for eight years. He had a sudden desire to touch it, feel its happy hours once again — but he was tormented by Pappa Lambro's haunting face.

He passed through the church again and hurried out the front door. A white dog was sniffing near the window of the butcher shop. It heard Stavro and ran off. Stavro stopped at Barba Spero's coffeehouse and looked back — the white dog was following him. He leaned down and patted it on the head. The dog arched its back affectionately against Stavro's leg while its tail worked furiously. They walked through the square together; a mangy half-starved dog, yet Stavro was drawing courage from it — sharing its last ounce of strength.

Unusual sounds were coming from the harbor; the sea could not calm herself. Caïques bounced loudly against each other, making weird echoes like the first tremors of an earthquake. Stavro paused at the cistern for a drink. First he cupped his hands together and offered some water to the dog. It took only a few licks. Suddenly a biting scream filled the night. Another! Stavro wiped his hands against the side of his trousers and ran across the square. The white dog barked gleefully and came chasing after him.

He saw three forms moving around the trunk of the plane tree — all of them women. With arms outstretched, heads up, they broke out into a second wave of wretched cries:

"Kostaki!"

"Nikko, my little Nikko!"

"Mitso — what have they done to you . . .?"

Standing directly beneath the tree now, Stavro brought his eyes up — a storm of nausea swelled inside his stomach: the huge tree was burdened with human bodies. They swayed and spun around in the strong wind, their heads tilted sharply to the side as if they had just heard a sound and were trying to make out what it was, from where it came . . . faces waxen in death, eyes bulging out, teeth clenched against lips, hands drooped.

There was no sign of Pappa Lambro!

The white dog leaped up and tried to play with one of the dangling feet. Stavro went to shoo it away; straightening up, something touched his head. He lifted his eyes and saw Pelopida's pain-wracked face staring down at him. Stavro let out a startled groan. He felt his knees giving in.

The cries mounted.

Lights went on in the houses; doors opened. Wide-eyed faces surrounded him . . . old women, children — all of them wailing, moaning, seeking vainly to speak into the dead ears

30

above them. The white dog was frightened and ran off. There was a deep silence and then a woman's shrieking voice fell on Stavro's ears:

"We have you to thank for this . . . you!"

Stravo felt a strong hand on his arm. He heard his uncle say, "Stavro, get away from here — quickly!"

Exhausted and confused, Stavro pushed him off. From the corner of his eye he saw Barba Spero bracing a ladder against the lowest branch of the tree. The old man climbed up, and with his soulia, began cutting at the rope that was holding Kostandi's head. The butcher's wife and two daughters came screaming for the body when it slumped to the ground. Barba Spero then swung the ladder to the next man: Nikko, the church sexton. Barba Spero worked on the rope for a long while before he could get Nikko to fall. Petro's hand again found Stavro's arm. "If you do not leave," he pleaded, "they will kill you!"

Now Barba Spero was working on Pelopida. He shifted hands with the soulia but after a few feeble strokes he went back to his right hand. When Pelopida at last started to fall Stavro ran to him and gathered him in his arms. With his uncle close at his heels Stavro carried the old man through the seething crowd, to the cistern. Carefully, he placed him against the wall in a sitting position, but Pelopida kept falling to the side like a puppet. . . . It was then that Stavro noticed the two placards pasted boldly on the wall of the cistern. One was printed in German, the other in Greek:

BY A DECISION OF THE GERMAN COURT MARTIAL OF 12 NOVEMBER 1942 TWENTY-SIX MALES OF PLATANO AND ITS ENVIRONS WERE SENTENCED TO

DEATH

BY HANGING, FOR THE MURDER OF THREE GERMAN SOLDIERS NEAR THE VILLAGE OF POTAMI, ON 10 NOVEMBER 1942. ALSO BY A DECISION OF THE

SAME COURT MARTIAL, EXECUTIONS WERE CAR-
RIED OUT IN THE FOLLOWING AREAS:

TRIPOLI	*107*	*males executed by shooting*
SPARTA	*86*	*males executed by shooting*
KALAMATA ..	*239*	*males executed by shooting*
ANDRITSA	*73*	*males executed by shooting*
MEGALOPOLIS	*94*	*males executed by shooting*
POTAMI	*11*	*males executed by hanging*

Tripoli, 12 November, 1942

THE FELDKOMMANDANT

For the third time Petro warned him: 'Stavro, in the name
of the Father — if you do not leave they will kill you!"
Stavro lifted Pelopida in his arms again and started up the
street with him. Looking back, he saw another man on the
ladder — Barba Spero was on his knees, one hand against
the trunk of the tree, vomiting. More faces sped past them
. . . mouths contorted, eyes terrified — all of them screaming their pain. Suddenly the church bell started in. Stavro
stopped in front of Barba Spero's coffeehouse. He eased Pelopida gently down alongside the window and wiped the sweat
from his face. His arms felt numb — his whole body ached.
In a rush of strength Petro reached down and lifted Pelopida.
He carried him toward the church with Stavro following.
Anna and the priest's wife were standing on the steps. The
priest's wife gave out a loud scream and came running toward
them, but when she realized it was Pelopida they were carrying, a look of relief settled over her face. Anna threw herself into Stavro's arms. "Where is Pappa Lambro?" she cried.
"I do not know," said Stavro.
"He is not on the tree," Petro said, hunching Pelopida close
to him once more. They walked across the street together.
Petro put the old man down on the first step of the church —

32

again Pelopida's body fell to the side. Stavro's eyes filled for the first time. "He always called me philosopher," he said to Anna.

She too began to cry. The priest's wife took Pelopida's head and stroked it tenderly with both hands. "The poor old man," she sobbed. "Why did they do this to him . . . why?"

The crowd had begun to move away from the plane tree — lines of mourners started marching toward the church, carrying the dead on wooden stretchers. As they drew near, an old woman bit her finger vindictively at Stavro:

"Murderer," she screeched. "Murderer!"

TWO

T HE DAY of Christ's birth!

Stavro lay on his cot, heavy-eyed, his mind rooted in Platano. He could not understand why on this day he should be obsessed with thoughts of Easter . . . he remembered with what joy the village would prepare itself — the houses got whitewashed, the bread baked, the eggs dyed, the lambs roasted; those happy visits to the little chapels high in the mountains . . . and then the Great Mass, the jubilant confusion of the Resurrection, muskets blasting away, the thunderous roar from the old cannon in the churchyard, the lighted candles rolling over the congregation like endless waves of newborn stars . . . finally Pappa Lambro's voice, cracked from strain and emotion, announcing to the world that Christ is Risen! A birth, a death, a Resurrection. Whole seasons losing themselves in flashes of time — vanishing in thin air before they are born. Days and years cramped together like lumps of deformity inside his heart, choking him, pinning him to the earth . . . chaining him there. It was this hungry power against which Stavro had always rebelled — this unrelenting force that could swallow everything: the four winds, the sea, heaven and earth . . . .

And now, less than an arm's length away, Pythagora lay gravely ill. Kapetan Thanasi was bent over the boy, feeling his pulse again. Looking grimly at Stavro, he said, "He is gone."

Every nerve in Stavro's body grew taut. Slowly Kapetan Thanasi pulled the heavy gray blanket over Pythagora's face. A thick cloud of gloom settled over the men. Kleanthi came and stood beside Pythagora. He placed his thin hand on the gray blanket, then withdrew it quickly. He did not know what to do with himself — he stood there nervously chewing his cheek . . . waiting perhaps for the first touch of dawn when other hands would help him lift Pythagora and carry him off . . . more than anything else dreading the final kiss, that last moment when the earth would tear itself open and engulf his friend forever . . .

"We are ready," said Kapetan Thanasi. "Put on your coat, Kleanthi." The boy gave him a blank look and walked toward his cot.

It made no sense to Stavro . . . a mother's anguished cry in the night, living flesh torn away from its womb, cast out by an angry God, and made to grope the earth with fingers still unborn . . . it made no sense to him at all!

"Will you read for Pythagora?" Kapetan Thanasi asked him.

"Kleanthi can do it," said Stavro.

"He is only a boy — he will cry and make a mess of it."

"Ask him."

"Stavro, I want you to do it."

"No," said Stavro, feeling the resentment mount up inside him. He walked to the fire and poured some coffee into his tin. Kapetan Thanasi stood close behind, waiting. "Stavro, please do it," he said.

"No!"

"For your soul's good. . . ."

Stavro laughed bitterly. He walked outside; it was snowing hard. He allowed the flakes to fall on his hot face. In a moment or two it would be dawn. Sky and earth, who had slept as lovers during the night, soon would stand naked before the world.

"I had no idea this would bother you so much," Kapetan Thanasi barked at him. Seeing that Stavro did not want to talk to him, he turned and went back to the cave. After a while, Stavro too returned. Panago was holding a shovel in his hand; he was the first to leave. Behind him came the others. They had Pythagora on a narrow stretcher, blanket and all. Kleanthi followed them out, tears streaming down his face, head down. Stavro walked out last.

When they reached a place inside the gorge where the earth was soft, Panago started digging. After he had gone a few feet he gave the shovel to Kapetan Thanasi, who leaped into the hole and began jabbing the shovel into the earth with great anger, as if it alone were responsible for Pythagora's death. He finished quickly, then stepped out of the hole. He motioned the others to ease Pythagora into the grave. As they did, the blanket slid away from the boy's face. Kleanthi burst into sobs. Kapetan Thanasi pulled the blanket back over Pythagora's face and held it until the stretcher settled in the grave.

A dull throb started pounding at Stavro's brain; it was as though he were looking down upon Stellio's open grave . . . above him, that day, huge black clouds soared, and a cold rain covered his face. Later, after they had returned home to eat the wheat of mourning, his mother stopped weeping long enough to tell them that Christ and the Virgin had loved Stellio so much they cried tears of rain for him. He did not answer her then but he wanted to. He had a savage desire to tell her that no one — neither in heaven nor earth, had the vaguest idea what had happened to Stellio, nor did they care. He wanted to tell her that God could not lift a finger to stop the rain, let alone breathe an ounce of life back into Stellio's parched lungs. . . .

3 6

"We cannot throw the boy into the ground without one word," Kapetan Thanasi grumbled under his breath, but Stavro heard him. Meanwhile, Panago was impatiently waiting to fill the hole. Kapetan Thanasi told him to begin. When the first spadeful of earth fell on Pythagora, Kleanthi groaned. His loud sobs brought tears into Stavro's eyes. It was here he felt the weightless touch of a finger on his heart. Trembling, he walked to the edge of the grave. Slowly, but with great force, he felt his lips moving, his mouth opening, his voice filling the gray silence:

The Lord is merciful and gracious,
slow to anger, and plenteous in mercy . . .
for as the heaven is high above the earth,
so great is His mercy toward them that
fear Him . . .

As far as the east is from the west,
so hath He removed our transgressions
from us . . .

For He remembereth that we are dust,
as for man, his days are like the grass,
as the flower of the field he flourisheth . . .
for the wind passeth over it and it is gone,
and the place thereof shall know it no more. . . ."

He could not go on. Tears choked him. He stepped back to let Panago finish with the shoveling. When at last the grave was filled, the men started walking slowly through the gorge, back to the cave. Stavro waited for Kleanthi — the boy stood hunched over the grave. He shoved a cross into the mound — two branches from a pine that he had carefully pared clean and knotted together with strong twine.

37

"Come, Kleanthi," said Stavro. "The others are waiting for us."

Something was bothering the boy. Dejectedly, he said to Stavro, "Tell me it is not true . . . what you said about man being only dust . . . tell me."

Stavro took his arm and lifted him to his feet. "Come, Kleanthi," he said.

But Kleanthi stood there, defiantly, "I want to know — tell me. Is Pythagora only dust . . . is he?"

The earth suddenly seemed to grow cold; the snow lost its purity. Taugetos appeared to shiver and shake, as though he were trying to sweep off centuries of pain. Now Kleanthi was fighting with his mouth again, striving to ward off a new surge of tears. "Pythagora whispered something to me last night," he said, "before he . . . before he died. He touched my face with his hot fingers and said, '*Kleanthi, I can see a beautiful place — it has tall purple mountains and wide green valleys. There are millions of flowers, Kleanthi . . . and the air has such a wonderful taste to it, so new and fresh, like the flutter of angels' wings . . . Look, Kleanthi, see how gracefully the gulls fly, how straight the cypresses grow, how blue the sea is . . . !*'"

"Come," said Stavro again. With shaking lips, Kleanthi said to him, "Is my father dust also . . . like Pythagora?"

Stavro pulled him forward. They passed silently through the gorge. Kapetan Thanasi was waiting for them outside the cave. "I was about to come after you," he told Stavro. "Is anything wrong?"

Stavro gave him a sour look. "Nothing is wrong," he said. "Nothing at all. . . ."

2

He had a deep longing to see Anna that night. He waited in the hills until vespers ended. Night fell quickly, bringing a raw breeze from the sea. He had to flail his arms and stamp his feet hard to keep the cold from his body, yet despite all this he could not push Pythagora from his mind, nor Kleanthi. He had a name for them: *Damon and Pythias* . . . friends unto death. And now only Pythias remained, like night cut off from day.

It was after nine o'clock when he entered the square. The priest's house lay in darkness. He crept around to the side and climbed the porch roof. He tapped softly on Anna's window. Nothing. He tapped again, louder. Cautiously, the curtain was rolled up. Anna opened the window. "Stavro . . ." she whispered.

"Keep your voice down."

"Is anything wrong . . .?"

"I have come to see you."

"It is late."

"I know, but I must talk with you, Anna."

"Come in . . . through the window."

"No . . ."

"My aunt is sleeping — she will not hear us."

Stavro climbed in. Her room smelled sweet and clean, as if a young child had been sleeping there. He kissed her lightly on the cheek. He opened his arms to her; she did not hesitate nor draw away. She wore only a woolen nightgown that hung loosely about her body. His mouth found hers. He dropped his hands to her thighs and with his fingers started pulling up on her nightgown. His hands touched her bare skin; hot flames seared his manhood. He kissed her again on the mouth. In a fit of impatience she wrestled out of the nightgown and clung to him, gasping for his mouth. He carried her to the bed.

"Anna," he sighed, "I have no right to touch you . . . there is guilt on my hands. Because of me hundreds have died. I killed them. That woman was right — I *am* a murderer. I murdered Pelopida . . . I murdered all the others. It is my

fault, my own fault, that Pappa Lambro is not with us today!"
His voice broke; he felt the tears flooding his eyes. But Anna
did not speak. She lay there breathing hard and twisting her
body. He forced his eyes away from her but she took his
hand in hers and placed it over her heaving breast. He eased
himself on the bed beside her. Still she did not speak.

Nor did she cry out when her moment came.

3

An hour later they both sat in the unlighted kitchen while
upstairs the priest's wife slept. A strange numbness crept over
Stavro's body. He tried not to think about it. Anna meanwhile could not take her eyes off him. She sat there in her
blue woolen robe, her hands outstretched, reaching for his.
The fire in the jaki died out, leaving only a faint glow from
the spitting embers. It threw a soft light on Anna's face, making her more beautiful than ever.

"I have loved you from the first day," she said to him.
"When you came here with Kapetan Thanasi to take communion."

"Can I not light a cigarette now?" he asked.

"No."

He put the cigarettes back in his pocket and leaned against
his chair. "I am hungry," he said. She went into the closet
and came back with half a loaf of hard bread and a small
end of white cheese. He fell on it quickly, stopping only to
offer her some, but she shook her head, smiling.

"Is there no wine?" he said.

"There is a little left in the barrel downstairs," said Anna,
getting up.

"No, it is too much trouble . . . your aunt might hear you."

"I will be quiet."

"Forget it." He went to the sink and drew a glass of water.
He could not drink it — it had a flat taste. He came back

40

and sat down while Anna wiped the table clean. The numbness was still in his body.

"Is there no one in the village who knows where Pappa Lambro could be?" he asked her.

She started to cry. He took her hand and squeezed it. "Why are you crying?" he said.

"Stavro . . . I am afraid."

"There is nothing to fear . . . the Germans will not harm him."

She was not really listening to him. As though in a deep trance, she said, "What do the Germans want with Greece? She is not beautiful any longer . . . She is starving, flies crawl over her body, her belly is swollen, her ribs stick out like rosary beads, she faints in the street and no one cares enough to pick her up . . . what do they want with her?"

"Anna, stop tormenting yourself."

That distant look of horror did not leave her face. ". . . Every night I pray to the Virgin — I beg Her to give us either bread or coffins . . ." Realizing too late what she said, she clamped both hands over her mouth. A hard lump of stone began forming inside Stavro's stomach.

"Your bread," he said. "I ate the last of your bread."

"No, Stavro — there is always more. A priest's house is never forsaken . . ."

"Anna, I should have known."

"We are in God's hands, Stavro — He will provide for us until Pappa Lambro returns."

Stavro felt the sourness mounting in his heart. "Anna," he said, "listen to me. I must tell you something . . . I have been afraid to look for Pappa Lambro."

"Stavro . . . !"

"All these weeks and I have done nothing."

"Why, Stavro?"

"When I was a boy, Anna, I loved God. Every Sunday I could not wait for the church to empty so that I might hurry

41

to the icons and kiss each saint's face. It was a beautiful world for me . . . I believed that God loved only me; that He threw His sun upon me every morning, and His stars at night. This is what I believed, Anna — God and I alone in the universe!"

She smiled at him but he took it wrongly. "Do not laugh at me, Anna. I will never forgive myself if I have caused Pappa Lambro to die also."

"Stop blaming yourself, Stavro."

". . . I have been afraid to look for him. I keep saying to myself: *'He is dead. He is dead!'* "

"No, Stavro — you *must* look for him. And you must look for God also. It is not too late to find Him."

"God does not exist for me . . . He never existed."

She smiled at him, "Stavro, can you not see God's finger leading me here to Platano . . . to you?"

"The Germans brought you here, not God!" he snapped. Instantly the words bit back at him. He took her into his arms and held her tightly. "Anna," he said, "do not expect anything from God. He cannot give you joy nor peace; nor can He fill your belly. He cannot do these things, Anna, because He died in your childhood!"

"No," she cried, whimpering. He waited for her to stop and then he lay with her, there on that cold kitchen floor while the fire from the jaki still sputtered weakly and her aunt's heavy snores filled the house.

4

A new year!

Once again he was in his mother's house. He came to her with no gifts this time, no guilt. He did something he had not done since he was a small boy — kissed her on the lips. Marika was overwhelmed. "What has come over you?" she said.

42

"I am hungry . . . is there anything in the house?"

"Only a few roots . . . I dug them out this morning."

"It does not matter," he said. "Perhaps I can find a fish or two on the quay." He reached for his khaki jacket.

"Stavro, listen to me — it is not safe to show your face in the village. They have not forgotten about Potami. . . ."

"I am not going to think about Potami any longer," he yelled at her. She lowered her eyes and said, "I am sorry, Stavro — I will not mention it again."

"How is Aunt Zacharo?" he said, stopping at the door.

"I am afraid she cannot last much longer."

"I will pass by and see her."

"Wait, I want to come with you," Marika said. She tossed her black shawl over her head and followed him out. A heavy rain was falling, splattering hard against the rooftops and forming large puddles in the street. Although his uncle's house was less than a stone's throw away, they were soaked to the skin when they got there. Petro let them in. Marika searched his eyes, looking perhaps for a faint glimmer of hope, but Petro turned and walked into the front room. Marika came after him. "How is Zacharo?" she asked. Petro stood by the window watching the rain pelt the square. His face had no expression as he said, "Pappa Thoma is reading over her. . . ."

"You summoned a priest?"

Petro spun around to look at Stavro. "Your aunt is dead," he said.

Marika rushed upstairs, sobbing. Stavro could not find any words to say to his uncle. He put his hand on Petro's shoulder and patted it many times. Half-chokingly, Petro said to him, "Now will you take me with you, Stavro?"

The priest came downstairs and joined them. He was a slight old man — bald and white-bearded. He offered Stavro his hand but Stavro shook it, he did not kiss it. Pappa Thoma gave him a penetrating stare. "Your aunt is in God's bosom," he said.

"I have nothing to give you, Pappa," said Petro apologetically. He threw on his jacket and started for the door, "Perhaps Barba Spero can come up with a little wine. . . ."

Pappa Thoma threw his hands up in protest. "I beg you," he cried, "you must not do this. Can you not see how dreadfully it is raining?"

"Pappa, where I come from it is a grave sin to show no hospitality to a stranger — let alone a priest!" With this Petro opened the door and ran out. Pappa Thoma took a chair beside the table and sat down. Glancing at Stavro, he said, "How old are you my son?"

"Twenty-three."

"You are not married?"

"No."

"Where do you keep yourself?"

"In the mountains . . . with Kapetan Thanasi."

The priest's face grew pale. "Were you with those who killed the three Germans?" he said.

"Yes."

Pappa Thoma crossed himself. "You must not reprimand yourself too severely, my son — it indeed was a high price to pay for only three Germans, but it had to be done." He was about to say something further, but Stavro stopped him.

"Pappa Thoma," he said, "have you heard anything about Pappa Lambro?"

The old priest's face brightened. He clapped his hands together and exclaimed, "In the name of the Virgin, my mind has run off with me. I have strong reason to believe that Pappa Lambro is in Kalavryta. . . ."

"Kalavryta?"

"Yes, a man from my village was there a few days ago. He heard in a coffeehouse that the Germans have a priest work-

44

ing with a crew of men, digging a road north of the city. . . ."

"What makes you think he is Pappa Lambro?"

"The Kalavrytans told this man that they were certain the priest came from the south, near Kalamata. . . ."

Stavro's heart leaped. Just then Petro came bursting in, drenched. He had a bottle in his hand. "You see, Pappa," he said, "God is good. He would never forgive me if I sent you away from my house empty-handed."

The priest smoothed down his beard while Petro went after the glasses. After Petro poured, they all touched glasses. Pappa Thoma cleared his throat and said, "Word of Life . . . may your wife's memory be eternal. . . ."

"Amen," said Petro, closing his eyes.

They drank. As soon as Petro drained his glass, a grin swept across his face. "Pappa," he said, "sorrow often makes the best of friends."

"Yes, and wine seals the friendship," the priest joyfully added.

"I have something to say to you, Pappa — about your village. We talk about you quite often — you have a reputation for being, let us say, frugal. Now the person who told me this swears it actually happened — it seems there was a man in your village whose name was Louka. He was a goatherd. He never bothered a soul — but when a man is peace-loving he is often taken for an idiot, is this not so?"

"Unfortunately, yes," said Pappa Thoma.

". . . One day Louka's wife got very sick. He tried everything: poultices, herbs, exorcisms, bloodletting . . . finally out of desperation, he called in the priest. Was it you, Pappa?"

"No — I am afraid this happened before my time." The priest seemed to be enjoying this and was quite impatient when Petro diverted from the story. "Go on," he said. "Go on!"

"Do not rush me — I do not want to bungle things . . ."

4 5

said Petro. "At last, Louka realized his wife was dying and there was nothing he could do for her. That night he went to the church and had a long talk with the Virgin. He got up early the next morning very determined — he dressed, shaved his face, took his mare and his rooster and walked nine miles to Sparta. When he came into the square he cried out: *'I am selling my mare . . . I am selling my mare!'* Soon a large crowd formed around him. One by one they examined the mare. They all agreed she was an excellent animal and asked Louka how much he wanted for her. *'Ten drachmas,'* said Louka. Everyone let out a roar and started to leave. *'Wait,'* yelled Louka, *'I am serious — who will buy my mare for ten drachmas . . . who?'* Finally one man stepped forward and said to Louka, *'For ten drachmas what have I to lose?'* He went to hand Louka the money but Louka said, *'No — whoever buys the mare must also buy the rooster.'* *'How much do you want for the rooster?'* said the man. *'A thousand drachmas,'* replied Louka. *'You poor ill-fated man,'* they all said to him. *'You have things slightly twisted — should it not be a thousand for the mare and ten for the rooster?'* But Louka was vehement, *'No,'* he cried *'ten for the mare . . . and a thousand for the rooster!'* At any rate, the man bought the mare subject to Louka's terms. Overjoyed, Louka took off his shoes and walked barefoot all the way back to Potami. His first stop was the church. He shoved the ten drachmas before the Virgin's face and cried, *'You see, Holy Mother, I have carried out my vow to you. I promised I would sell my mare and give the money to you and the church . . . now, you must carry out your end of the bargain and cure my wife, Elpiniki. . . .'* "

The glasses were empty again. Petro filled them; he was about to launch into something else when Marika came downstairs. Red-eyed, she threw Petro a severe look. "Stories . . . at a time like this?"

"Blame me, my child," said Pappa Thoma. "It was my fault. . . ."

Marika turned to Stavro, "Are you not coming upstairs?" she snapped.

"No," he said, fingering his glass.

"Why not?"

"There is nothing to see . . . nothing."

5

It was through Tigani the train would pass. That night they all sat around the fire waiting for the soup to boil. They had a new mouth to feed: Petro. The day after the funeral he came to Stavro's house and slept there, to make certain Stavro would not leave without him. And now he was here, inside the cave, talking with Kapetan Thanasi as though he had known him all his life.

"Friend Kapetan," he was saying, "these forty-eight-year-old eyes of mine have seen many things. Nothing escapes them. I have learned one valuable lesson from life — I call it the rule of the scale. Yes, life is a scale . . . you tip up one end and down goes the other — to gain a wife you lose a mother, to gain a child you lose a wife, to gain the eternal you must lose everything. This is life . . . profit and loss."

"What are you trying to tell us?" said Kapetan Thanasi.

"This, friend Kapetan — a while back you lost one gun, is this not so?"

"One gun?"

"I speak of Pythagora. . . !"

"I understand."

"You see . . . the scale tilted. Now you must bring it back to level again."

"How?" said Kapetan Thanasi.

"By replacing the gun you lost. You cannot hide from the

scale, friend Kapetan — I have been sent here by fate to take Pythagora's place."

"You have thirty years on Pythagora."

"Thirty years of experience . . . I have eaten from the jar of life with a large spoon."

"Did you fight the Italians in Albania?" said Kapetan Thanasi.

"No."

"The Germans . . . in Macedonia and Thrace?"

"No."

"You did not serve in the army?"

"No, I was sick, friend Kapetan."

"Sick?"

"I am not ashamed to expose my soul to you, friend Kapetan — I saw the Italians and Germans coming and I shit in my pants. It is as simple as that."

Kapetan Thanasi stepped back as though suddenly blinded by an evil flame, but this did not bother Petro. "Have you so quickly forgotten what I said about the scale, friend Kapetan?" he exclaimed. "Listen to me — when the Italians and Germans climbed into our country I got so frightened I did not know what to do with myself. Can you imagine my shame, seeing my own brother, my friends and neighbors, all of them marching off in uniform while I wallowed in my fear. Nothing can tilt your scale more than this, friend Kapetan. . . ."

"He is a coward!" yelled Stavro, enraged.

"My nephew is right . . . yes, I am a coward . . . I am full of shit . . . my own shit . . . my own stinking shit!" Petro covered his eyes with both hands.

"There is no need for this," barked Kapetan Thanasi, glaring at Stavro. "Your uncle came here in all sincerity — we must hear him out."

"I tell you he is a coward. I know him . . . I have lived with him. You must send him back!"

48

Petro fell on his knees before Kapetan Thanasi. "In the name of the Father, friend Kapetan — do not cast me away!" he cried.

"Enough!" Kapetan Thanasi pulled Petro sharply to his feet. Glancing fiercely at Stavro again, he said, "I did not expect this from you. He is your father's brother . . . your own flesh and blood. I am not concerned how he lived his life — he came here to help us and, God knows, we need him. I cannot send him away." He turned to Petro. "Friend Petro, take my hand in yours . . . swear you will never let it go until the last German leaves Greece."

"I swear," choked Petro. Kapetan Thanasi kissed him on the cheek; the other men did the same. Stavro refused to move. With mounting disgust he watched his uncle embrace each man. Stavro had to get away.

Outside, the sky glittered with stars, suspended high above his head like countless diamonds — held there it seemed by only thin strands of air. Any moment now they could let go and come crashing to the earth. If Pappa Lambro were here he would probably say to him it was God's hand that held them . . . God's eye that made them sparkle. *Pappa Lambro! He was hounding Stavro . . . hounding him.*

A voice fell on his back. He saw his uncle walking toward him. "Stavro, are you not going to shake my hand?"

Stavro turned his back on him.

"Kapetan Thanasi said I could go to Tigani tomorrow."

Stavro took out a cigarette and lit it.

"Are you angry with me, Stavro?"

"No," Stavro lied.

"I did not want to cause any ill feeling between you and Kapetan Thanasi. . . ."

Stavro turned and walked into the cave. The soup was ready: a few beans, herbs . . . boiled in water. Stavro could not finish it. He saw Kleanthi staring at him. Stavro gave him his tin of soup and watched as the boy gulped it down. Petro

49

came and sat beside them. "Stavro," he said, "will there be any trouble at Tigani tomorrow?"

"I do not know."

"This is the first time I have been away from home, Stavro. . . ."

"You had better not make a mess of things," Stavro warned him.

"I am sleepy," said Petro. 'Where is my bed?"

Stavro pointed to Pythagora's cot. Petro went to it and sat down just as Kapetan Thanasi began playing softly on his mandolin. A few of the men joined in with the words:

> Black is the night on the mountains,
> snow is falling in the rocks . . .
> and in the dark wilderness
> the Klepht is drawing out his sword.

After a while Stavro too climbed into his cot. At first he could not sleep. Tigani was foremost in his mind: Two thousand Greek prisoners stuffed inside a German train . . . a quick stop for water . . . five minutes, this was all the time they had . . . !

He was about to close his eyes when he felt a heavy hand on his shoulder. "Stavro . . . you will stay near me tomorrow?" Petro whimpered.

"Go to sleep!"

"I cannot shut my eyes. . . ."

"Keep your voice down."

"Stavro, do you remember that night when the snake crawled into your bed . . . ?"

"Yes."

"You were sleeping in my house . . . you were such a young boy, Stavro. Things were so different then — your father was alive, and Stellio was only a baby . . . time does terrible things to us . . . terrible things!"

50

"Must you speak so loudly?"

" . . . I can remember that snake so clearly, Stavro — it was a tiny black one. You came running downstairs holding it in your hands. You said it felt very cold and you asked me if you could keep it in bed with you . . . to warm it. Do you not remember, Stavro?"

"Yes, I remember."

"You liked me then, Stavro — you liked me very much. You always came to visit us . . . in the name of Christ, why do things have to change?"

"Uncle Petro — please go to sleep."

"You have not called me that for a long time. . . ." Petro reached out his hand. "Hold me, Stavro," he said. "Hold my hand as you did when you were a small boy. . . ."

Hating himself, Stavro took his hand — it felt cold and sweaty. Just then, he recalled clearly his Aunt Zacharo's words from her deathbed: *"Stavro, take your uncle with you . . . do it for me and Christ will bless you!"*

6

They started out early in the morning, moving past a jagged corridor of isolated rock, into a nest of hills. The sky seemed anxious to unburden itself of more snow — dense gray clouds clenched themselves together in one huge fist and looked menacingly at the earth below. By mid-morning Kapetan Thanasi had led them across a wide rock-strewn valley, stopping to rest beside a wild fig tree. A thin vein of water hemorrhaged nearby. Stavro sat on a rock beneath the tree and lit a cigarette while the others drank. Panting hard, Petro said to Kapetan Thanasi, "How far is Tigani from here?"

"Two, three cigarettes," replied the Kapetan. They moved on, across a bleached-out watershed, and up another gaping wall of rock. Petro touched Stavro on the back. "Nephew," he said, "you did something back there that can never be forgiven. . . ."

Stavro lit another cigarette. Panago overheard Petro and said, "What did he do?"

"He sat in the shade of a fig tree. . . ."

"So?"

"Do you not know that a fig tree is a cursed thing and its shade can drive a man insane?"

"Goatshit!" yelled Panago. "What is so evil about a poor little fig tree?"

"I will answer you, friend Panago — but first tell me — have you ever read the Bible?"

"Once or twice."

"Then you must know that Christ performed many miracles while He was here on earth?"

"Of course."

"Perhaps you do not remember this, but one day Christ was returning home from work, tired and hungry. From afar He saw a fig tree; His mouth watered as He ran toward it. But when He got there He found it had no figs on it. Friend Panago, Christ got so angry, He swore. Yes, He let out a curse and cried, *'Wicked fig tree, you have no idea how much I hungered for one of your figs. I place this curse upon you — from this day on, you shall never bear another fig . . . I shall see to it personally!'*

"Goatshit!" cried Panago.

"I tell you, friend Panago, that poor ill-fated fig tree dropped its barren little arms almost to the ground and fig tears, the size of your hand, began oozing from its branches."

"Goatshit!"

Stavro tossed the stub of his cigarette away and lit another. He saw Kleanthi edging his way toward him, his thin shoulder stooped from the weight of his rifle. "Stavro," he said, "I must ask you something."

"What is it?"

"I want to know where you learned those words. . . ."

"What words?"

"I mean, what you said when we buried Pythagora. . . ."

"Stop thinking about Pythagora!"

"Are you afraid to tell me?"

"Of course not."

"Stavro, I have been thinking about them for days — at first they bothered me, but now I realize how beautiful they are: *'The Lord is merciful and gracious, slow to anger, and plenteous in mercy . . .'* I never understood God to be this way."

Stavro took one final puff from his cigarette and tossed it away. They stopped to rest again on the summit of a high slope. Below them, wedged snugly between two towering flanks of Taugetos, lay Tigani — its few dozen white houses gleaming against the dark sky. As they started down the slope Stavro glanced at his uncle — Petro was talking to Panago in a calm voice. Stavro drew away from Kleanthi and went to join them. Now that they were at Tigani's door he knew he would have to keep a close eye on his uncle. Petro seemed unruffled; he slapped Panago jokingly on the back and said to him, "Friend Panago, have you ever thought about death . . . do you wonder sometimes what is to become of us when that frightful moment arrives?"

"You speak of death too loosely," said Panago. "Only madmen and monks talk this way."

"Then you have not given it much thought?"

"No."

"This is a sad mistake, friend Panago. Let me ask you this: When the Italians invaded Greece did you join or wait to be drafted?"

"I joined!"

"Exactly. It is the same way with death . . . one must not sit idly by and wait to be called. What I am trying to say is we should be prepared for death. Speaking for myself, I have already chosen my work for the next life. . . ."

"You *are* a madman," cried Panago.

Petro went on: "Yes, friend Panago, I have my heart set on being the chief policeman of heaven. I feel I am qualified for the job — I have been a goatherd most of my life. I know what it is to maintain order, how to separate the bad from the good. May I ask you, friend Panago, what sort of work you have done?"

"I was a butcher in Kalamata."

"A butcher, did you say? This presents a serious problem . . . in heaven, there is no meat — only souls and spirits . . . if you follow me, friend Panago?"

"I follow you."

"Perhaps you can learn a new trade — you are still a young man," Petro said. Getting uncomfortable, Panago pointed his thumb toward Stavro. "What about him?" he asked. "What will his job be?"

"My nephew? Have you not noticed, friend Panago, his inordinate love for smoke and flame — the cigarette never leaves his mouth. Stavro's job is secure . . . he shall be the Prometheus of heaven!"

"Who was Prometheus?"

"Your brain is in deplorable condition, friend Panago."

"I am a butcher — not a bookworm!"

"Do you not know that a man cannot live by meat alone?"

"Give me meat, Barba — you and your nephew can chew on words."

Petro put a firm hand on Panago's shoulder. "Friend Panago," he said, "where I come from, a Barba is an old man. I do not want you to call me that again — do you understand?"

They were entering the village now. A group of children came running to meet them, screaming and waving their hands. Stavro touched his uncle on the back and said, "Are you all right?"

Petro spun around defiantly. "I feel wonderful, nephew . . . I cannot wait to pull this trigger!" He fingered his rifle nervously while his eyes flicked from one house to the other. The church bell started in. More faces appeared in the street. A young boy approached them. Petro took hold of his arm and asked him, "What is your name, little goat?"

"Stellio," said the boy.

Stavro's eyes watered instantly. He kneeled down and embraced the boy, then lifting him up, he continued walking.

"Little goat, where do you live?" said Petro.

"There, next to the church," replied the boy. He snuggled happily into Stavro's arms. A train of children followed enviously behind.

"Is your father at home?" Petro asked the boy.

"Yes."

"And your mother?"

"Yes . . . my brother and two sisters also."

Panago overheard this and said, "Your two sisters, are they older than you?"

"Much older."

"Little goat, tell me," said Petro, pushing Panago away, "does your father have any wine in his cellar?"

"I think so."

Petro crossed himself. Glancing at Stavro, he yelled, "Prometheus, the scale is tilting . . . God is about to fill our bellies. In the name of the Father, listen to those bells . . . I feel like Christ entering Jerusalem!"

7

It seemed the whole village crammed itself into the little Church of the Assumption later that afternoon. The old priest, Pappa Demetrios, quickly skipped through vespers and after reading the prayer of Simeon, he crossed himself three times and climbed the ambon. He was slight and bald, stoop-shouldered. He had a habit of stroking his gray-forked beard before speaking. "Beloved Christians," he said, "our village has been blessed with visitors. I need not remind you that these men sacrifice their lives every day, denying themselves even the basic joys of family, relatives, and friends. Their reward can come only from our Lord and Savior, Jesus Christ, who said: *'He who sacrifices his life shall find it, and he who saves his life shall lose it.'* God has led these men to us . . . we must open our hearts to them, invite them into our homes, offer them what little food we have, and give them our beds. But they did not come here merely to eat and sleep . . . I have asked their Kapetan to talk to you. I beg you now to join hands with him and listen to every word he has to say. . . ."

Kapetan Thanasi walked to the ambon, crossed himself and began: "Holy Father, beloved people of Tigani — my heart trembles as I stand here in the sight of God and His saints. At nine o'clock tomorrow morning, a train carrying two thousand Greek prisioners will stop here for water. It will be heavily guarded. I need not tell you that these prisoners will be on their way to German labor camps where they will be forced to drain out the rest of their days. Sooner or later, we must all do something for our country . . . we cannot escape it. Tigani's hour has come. Your village stands in dire peril; you may all lose your lives, but this train must be stopped. The prisoners must be freed!"

There was a long moment of silence. Finally a man spoke out. "I am Theotoki Ladas . . . although my name implies that I work with olives and oil, in truth I am a miller — I have the only flour mill from here to Sparta. . . ."

Pappa Demetrios stroked his beard and cut in on him. "Get on with it, Theotoki," he shouted. "We do not care to hear about your worldly achievements."

Theotoki suddenly grew uneasy, as though the full realization of addressing an audience had just struck him. His face got white and pockmarked with sweat; he was about to stop but he shook his head twice and struggled on. "I am a miller — not a speaker. Yes, my heart also overflows with patriotism . . . my great great-grandfather fought alongside Kolokotroni. I have

56

his sword at home to prove it . . . I do not want anyone here to misunderstand me, but why must the train be attacked in our village? Surely there are other stops . . . why us? Why Tigani?"

"That is a fair question," said Kapetan Thanasi. "The answer is quite simple: your village was chosen because it is the first stop. The element of surprise is one advantage we cannot afford to lose. The Germans will not expect trouble so soon."

"They may kill us all," cried Theotoki. "They can burn our homes . . . destroy everything!"

"Yes," said Pappa Demetrios, frowning, "our homes, our sheep, our goats . . . even your rich flour mill, Theotoki."

Theotoki sat down. An old woman cried out, "It is far better to have one moment of freedom than five hundred years of slavery!"

The others in the church took up her call, *"Freedom or Death . . . Freedom or Death!"* In one voice they began singing the hymn to the Virgin.

Later, outside the church, Petro took hold of Kapetan Thanasi's arm and said to him, "That was a good speech you made, friend Kapetan. However, you were standing so low, no one could see you. Why did you not climb up the ambon?"

Kapetan Thanasi grinned. Stavro lit a cigarette. The church emptied quickly — Pappa Demetrios came out, still wearing his robes. Stavro helped him down the steps. The priest touched him jubilantly on the shoulder and cried, "They are with us — every last one of them!"

"The miller too?" said Stavro.

"Theotoki also," Pappa Demetrios replied. Looking at Stavro closely, he said, "Where are you sleeping tonight, my son?"

"I do not know yet."

"You are coming with me . . . to my house."

As soon as Stavro accepted, he regretted it. He could not understand this strong compulsion: running to a priest every chance he got.

When he told Petro where he was going he wanted to come

also, but Stavro made him go with Kapetan Thanasi. "I shall see you in the morning," Stavro told him.

Petro sulked, head down.

"Do you need anything?" Stavro said.

"No."

"If you want me for some reason, you know where I will be. . . ."

"Do not concern yourself," his uncle replied sourly, "I have nursed this body for forty-eight years."

"Goodnight," said Stavro.

"Goodnight, Prometheus."

He awoke with the church bell early the next morning. The priest's wife already had the coffee on the jaki. Pappa Demetrios was sitting at the kitchen table, wrestling with his thoughts. They ate silently. After breakfast Pappa Demetrios took out a small bottle of wine and poured two glasses. "This is the last of it," he said to Stavro. "I do not know what I shall do for Sunday — there is not a drop left in the whole village. How can I give communion . . . ? But God provides . . . I must not worry about tomorrow — *sufficient for the day is the evil thereof. . . .*"

"Your Grace. . . ."

"Yes, my son — speak."

"Why did you become a priest?"

Stunned for a moment, Pappa Demetrios placed his empty glass on the table. "Why does anyone become a priest?" he exclaimed. "To serve God, and man!"

"No," said Stavro. "It is impossible — one cannot serve God and man at the same time. . . ."

The old priest looked at him kindly and said, "My son, we are all God's children, made in His image and likeness. By loving each other, we serve God."

"You did not answer my question. I want to know why you, *Pappa Demetrios,* became a priest. Did you feel God's finger

5 8

on your soul . . . did His voice speak into your heart . . . ?"

Pappa Demetrios laughed. "I would be the last to put such a decision in God's hand. Yes, at times we priests like to delude ourselves into thinking we are called by God — but in my case this is not so. I alone am answerable. I chose the priesthood with my eyes wide open. . . ."

"You honestly feel you are serving mankind?"

"Yes."

". . . with vespers, holy water, and fastings?"

"Yes," replied the priest, looking at him sternly now. His wife got up and left the room. Stavro put on his jacket and walked to the door.

"You did not finish your wine," said Pappa Demetrios.

Stavro stood facing the door. "I am sorry if I upset you," he said. The priest too got up; he placed his hand on Stavro's head. "No man can fight God," he whispered. "It is an uneven match. Give your soul peace — accept Christ. I promise you, life will take on a new meaning for you."

Stavro opened the door and walked outside. The priest came with him as far as the street. When Stavro would not take his hand to kiss it, he lifted his fingers and blessed him. "Go to the Good, my son — God protect you . . . may He bring you quickly into His arms."

Kapetan Thanasi and the others were waiting for him on the steps of the church. It seemed the whole village was there also. The young girls came flocking around Kleanthi, giggling at each other, and edging their way closer to him. Red-faced, he was happy to see Stavro. "You are late," he stammered. "Kapetan Thanasi was about to come after you."

"Where is my uncle?" Stavro asked him.

"In the rocks, behind the church — he drank much wine last night. . . ."

"He is not ill?"

"No, he has the runs," Kleanthi said and laughed.

Kapetan Thanasi moved in between them. "Did you sleep well?" he asked Stavro.

"Yes."

"I have changed our plans — your uncle shall be with you, Kleanthi, and Panago. I take the others . . . four on one side of the tracks, five on the other. Keep twenty-five meters away from each other, and conceal yourselves well in the rocks."

"Does he have to come with me?"

"Yes — he begged me . . . he wants to be near you, he said. Stavro, are you listening to me?"

"I heard you."

"No one must expose himself, do you understand?"

"Yes." From behind the church Stavro saw his uncle walking toward them slowly. Petro's eyes were puffed and red. "Good morning, Prometheus," he mumbled.

"How do you feel?" said Stavro.

"Drained. Flushed out. That was bad wine I drank last night . . . bad wine."

"Are you certain it was wine?"

"I know what you are thinking . . . that I am shitting in my pants again. But you are wrong — it *was* the wine. What did the ancients say . . . *A man is happy only when he keeps his bowels open and his mouth shut?* I am halfway to happiness, Prometheus . . . yes, halfway!"

Pappa Demetrios came out of the church, holding a gold-plated Bible high in his hands. He lifted his eyes toward the tower and nodded — instantly the bell started clanging.

"Hey, what is this — a feast day?" Panago yelled. "Tell that fool priest to stop ringing that bell — every German within fifty miles will hear it!"

Marching slowly, the priest led his people out of the church-yard, into the street. When they came to the cistern they formed a circle around Pappa Demetrios and began singing:

> *When Gabriel saw the beauty*
> *of Your virginity,*

and Your immaculate purity . . .
he cried out in awe:
What can I say to praise Thee?
What name shall I give Thee?
I am speechless, and full of doubt . . .
and can say only,
Hail, Thou full of grace!

Petro slapped Kapetan Thanasi on the back and shouted, "In the name of the Father — are we going on a pilgrimage?"

"Let them sing," said the Kapetan. "They are doing us no harm."

Panago threw up his hands in disgust. "Is this their secret weapon . . . is this how they intend to help us?"

"Kyrie eleison!" cried Petro.

Stavro went to the cistern and took a long drink. Pappa Demetrios stood by, waiting for him to finish. "You will soon discover," he said, patting Stavro fondly on the head, "that the work of a priest is not confined to Kyrie eleisons, holy water, and fastings. Here, my son, kiss the gold Bible . . . we are about to begin."

"What do you mean?" said Stavro.

"You asked for our help and we shall give it."

Stavro became alarmed. "Your Grace, we will never forgive ourselves if anything happens to you. Please be careful."

Pappa Demetrios, forgetting he had asked Stavro to kiss the Bible, turned and hurried back to his flock. Knots of children formed around the cistern and started splashing water at each other. The priest made them stop. Suddenly Kapetan Thanasi knelt down and placed one ear on the railroad track. He leaped to his feet. "Quickly, the train is coming . . . to your places!"

Still clutching his gold Bible with one hand, Pappa Demetrios crossed himself and stepped boldly forward, stopping alongside the tracks. Stavro grabbed Kleanthi by the arm and pulled him into the rocks. Petro doggedly kept at their heels. Panago found his place and squatted behind a large rock. Im-

61

patiently he motioned them away from his range. Now Kleanthi buried himself between two huge boulders and sat there, trembling. Before moving on, Stavro waited for his uncle. Petro crawled forward a few paces, then dropped to his knees, white with fear.

"Get up!" Stavro yelled at him.

The train came steaming toward the village, blowing great puffs of black smoke into the sky. Petro moaned and rolled over the ground; he threw a helpless look at Stavro. "Go to your place," he cried. "I will be all right in a minute . . . !"

Stavro went to pull him to his feet but Petro let out an agonizing cry and started vomiting, drenching Stavro's jacket. Stavro left him there, heaving and clawing at the ground. He hid behind some rocks just as the train screeched to a halt near the cistern.

German soldiers leaped out — a half-dozen from each car. With automatic rifles up, they groped the earth and sky while more soldiers poured out of the train. They carried buckets and formed a long line to the cistern. In quick precision they filled the buckets and carried them to the engine where they were funneled in by two soldiers standing on a makeshift platform. Meanwhile Pappa Demetrios and his flock, still bunched together alongside the tracks, began waving at the faces in the windows of the train. Now, they began singing the anthem. The Germans went on with their work, ignoring them. When they finished, the soldiers with the buckets were the first to climb back on the train, then the guards — six at a time. After the last German got on, the engine let out a fierce blast. Another. Suddenly Pappa Demetrios raised his hands. The singing stopped. Calmly he took off his kalimafi and flung himself over the tracks, still clutching his gold Bible. Others quickly followed. Soon, every last one of his congregation lay stretched across the tracks, some of them piled on top of others.

Two Germans jumped from the train. One pointed his automatic rifle at the priest's head and ordered him to get up, but

Pappa Demetrios refused to move. More Germans came leaping out. An officer pulled free his revolver and aimed it at the priest. Just then, a flurry of rifle shots filled the air.

Kapetan Thanasi!

The German officer fell to the ground, screaming. The soldiers turned and ran for the cars but before they could climb up, Stavro, Panago, and Kleanthi opened fire. *Somehow it did not bother Stavro . . . killing Germans from a distance.* Not one of them could get back into the train. Now the engine howled once more. It pushed forward, into the mass of people, striking them hard . . . relentlessly, viciously, until it could go no further. Like a wounded beast, it pulled back, then rammed forward once again.

Stavro could bear no more. He tugged free one of his grenades and hurled it under the engine. The blast was deafening. More soldiers streamed from the train but the rifles met them head-on. A second wave of soldiers gushed out — they fled down the tracks toward the distant hills, leaving their prisoners unguarded.

Five minutes passed without a shot being fired.

A jubilant voice cried out, "They are gone . . . the Germans have run off!"

Heads popped out of the train . . . Greek heads! They rushed toward the villagers, pulled them to their feet, and embraced them. They kissed cheeks, slapped each other on the back, shouted at one another hoarsely. Stavro eased his way out of the rocks. He was the first to reach the priest, who was still lying across the tracks, not moving. Kneeling down, Stavro placed his ear over his heart. There was no life in it. Tears flooded Stavro's eyes. He felt Kapetan Thanasi's hand on his shoulder.

"Is he dead?"

"Yes."

"Five others were crushed also," said Kapetan Thanasi.

"They are dead?"

"Yes."

Stavro's voice shook. "Was it the grenade?"

"I said they were crushed."

Again Stavro bent over the priest. Pappa Demetrios' chest and face were soaked with blood. His eyes were still open and glaring frightfully at the ground; the gold Bible lay at his side unharmed. Stavro got up and walked to the cistern. He tossed a handful of water over his burning face. As he went to dry it with the back of his hands he saw his uncle coming slowly toward him. Stavro suddenly realized the smell of the man still lay heavily on his jacket. In a fit of anger he tore the jacket off his back and flung it to the ground just as Petro reached his side. With a detestable grin he said to Stavro, "Prometheus ... we won ... we won!"

THREE

THE FIRST hours of spring.

Full-grown and strong once again, the sun began melting the snows on Taugetos; the earth gave birth to new seeds, new hopes. A whole winter passed and Stavro had not taken one step toward Kalavryta. Remorse-stricken, he tried to justify himself many times, but always it was Anna . . . he could not keep away from her. Night after night his hungry arms found her — either in her bedroom, or on the sofa in the front room. Once, when the priest's wife could not sleep and sat nervously beside the jaki muttering faint words and nodding her sad head, they walked to the quay together in a soaking rain. Inside a deserted fishing shack Anna took off her coat and dried her face and hair with a handkerchief. Although the floor was damp and cold, and a shivering wind swarmed into the shack from the sea, Stavro clasped her trembling body to his and took her as they stood on their feet, for he had a great desire. That night, Anna too forgot about Kalavryta.

"Hold me, Stavro," she whispered.

"Anna . . ."

"Do not say a word — just hold me."

"Anna, listen to me . . . I must go to Kalavryta."

"No," she sighed, and he caught her biting her lip as she said it.

"It will only be for a few days," he said.

"No!" She held him tighter now. "I do not want to lose you, Stavro . . . as I lost my mother and father, my sister and brothers. . . ."

"I made a promise, Anna — do not keep me from it."

With great fear in her eyes she begged him, "Stavro, wait until the spring."

"Why?"

"I shall be certain then . . . that I can give you a child."

"Anna . . ."

She started to cry, softly as though she found relief from her words. He waited for her to stop before embracing her again. She gave him her mouth, her body. She made a ritual of it, this Minoan princess — never fully satisfied the first time, she always needed him twice. It was so that rainy night in the fishing shack. Forced to remain on their feet, they found it awkward and difficult, yet they persisted, driven by savage hunger. And when finally and ecstatically they discovered each other again, it was Anna who let out the first cry. Anna, who had always kept her world hidden, even from him . . . slumped in his arms like a tired sheep, gasping into his ear, imploring him to fill the void in her womb.

Today, Stavro made up his mind.

He dressed quickly, washed his face and waited for the coffee. It would not be an easy matter convincing Kapetan Thanasi — Stavro had willingly joined hands with him, vowed never to leave him even unto death. Wedged between an oath and a promise, he did not know which way to turn, but before another thought could enter his mind he felt his uncle's hand on his shoulder.

"You look pale this morning," Petro told him.

Stavro turned to leave.

"Wait, I must speak to you," Petro cried out in a choking

66

voice. "Stavro, you have avoided me since ... since Tigani."
He spun Stavro around and held him by both arms. "I tried,
Stavro ... I tried. I did not want to get sick at Tigani — if you
only knew how much I prayed to God to help me. In the name
of the Father, you must believe me, Stavro!"

"I have nothing to say to you!" yelled Stavro.

Petro's eyes watered. He followed Stavro to the fire; he
stood beside him as Stavro poured some coffee into his tin,
then with a hollow groan, he said, "Killing comes easy for you
... you pull the trigger and *pfft,* it is over. No fear, no
trembling, no loose shit gushing through your bowels like mad
water, no guilt to stain your soul. Twice have I killed, Stavro
— in forty-eight years I screwed up enough courage to kill
twice. Once, when I was a boy of ten while walking in the hills
behind my house, I saw a tiny sparrow flitting its wings in a
stagnant pool of water. It was so happy it did not hear me ...
it did not see me pick up a stone and hurl it flush against its
little chest. Yes, I killed it. . . ."

"Why are you telling me this?" Stavro glared at him. But
Petro plowed on, ". . . the second time was more difficult, I
was fifteen, a giant of a lad, always in the hills with my father's
goats, sleeping on the cold ground with them, a glutton for hard
work. We had a dog, a bitch ... her name was Nausica. How
she loved those goats! Stavro, please listen to me ... she
watched over them like a hawk. One day a male dog caught
her in season and gave her a litter of puppies — nine of them,
black and white like Nausica. She nursed them night and day,
that is all but one. This she picked up by the scruff of its neck
and hid it under a pile of dirt in a corner of the cellar. I could
not understand why she did this. With tears flooding my eyes
I heard my father explain it was a sickly puppy and would
soon die. I begged him to save the ill-fated thing but he answered, *'There is only one way to help it: a merciful death.'*
I fell into sobs and said no, but he ordered me to take the
puppy to the stream behind the rocks and hold its little head

67

under the water for a few minutes. I could not sleep for a whole week after that — neither could I eat, nor work with the goats in the hills. Even today, I close my eyes and see that ill-fated puppy under the clear water, its tiny mouth wide open gasping for air, its eyes horrified at the sight of death. . . !"

Stavro turned to walk away but Petro took hold of his arms again. "It is not easy for me to kill, Stavro."

"I must see Kapetan Thanasi," said Stavro coldly.

"Stavro, do not leave yet."

"There is nothing further to say."

"I can learn to kill, if you will help me, Stavro."

The others were awake. Kapetan Thanasi was bent over the water pan washing his face. Panago stood behind him, waiting. Kleanthi saw Stavro and came toward him.

"Leave us, little goat," said Petro. "Can you not see I am speaking to my nephew?"

Face downcast, Kleanthi moved off. Petro waited a long time before going on. "When your aunt was sick, I had terrible fears . . . many nights I trembled in bed, a cold sweat drenching my body. I tell you it was agony waiting for her to die. But once it happened, Stavro, it did not frighten me any longer. That same night I walked all those kilometers to Potami and summoned the old priest. After that I had many things to think about . . . the wake, the funeral, the relatives and friends who flocked to my house after the burial . . . Death is never as we dread it to be, Stavro — can killing be the same?"

Stavro left him there, mumbling to himself. Kapetan Thanasi was still rubbing his face vigorously with the towel — he had not seen Stavro yet. For a long while Stavro watched him: he was like a block of marble, cold and hard . . . half-shepherd, half-king . . . Cleobis or Biton emerged from eternal sleep, about to pull the universe across the earth's dusty face . . . massive shoulders, bull neck, powerful legs . . .

From behind the towel he saw Stavro and smiled, "Good morning."

Stavro nodded.

"Have you had coffee yet?"

"Yes."

"Stavro, do you not know what day this is?"

Stavro looked at him glumly. It seemed Christ was born only yesterday . . . four short months between a breath and a death . . . and now He was about to be crucified once more, not by the Romans and Jews, but by pageantry and splendor, by candles, red eggs, muskets, and sanctimonious cries: *"He is Risen! He is Risen!"*

"Are you not going to wish me a Good Resurrection?" said Kapetan Thanesi. But Stavro, still submerged in his thoughts, did not answer him.

"We are all going to Potami — to church," said Kapetan Thanasi.

"Today?"

"Yes."

"Kapetan Thanasi, I want to ask you something. . . ."

"Later, after the Resurrection."

"No — it has to be now."

"Speak then."

"I must go to Kalavryta. . . ."

"What?"

"Pappa Lambro may be a prisoner there — the old priest of Potami said that one of his parishioners was in Kalavryta recently. He overheard someone in the coffeehouse say a priest from the south was working with a crew of men, digging out a road. . . ."

"But you are not certain if this is Pappa Lambro?"

"I must go there and find out."

"Kalavryta is more than one hundred kilometers from here — do you expect to get there without any trouble from the Germans?"

"I must," said Stavro.

"I cannot let you go."

69

"I said I must!"

"If you take one step, I will shoot you . . . in the name of the Father, I swear I will kill you!"

Petro overheard them. "Why all the noise?" he asked. "Hey, friend Kapetan — did my nephew say something to upset you . . . did he?"

"Your nephew places very little value on his head!" Kapetan Thanasi barked at him with a ferocious look.

"Aman, I have told him this many times, friend Kapetan — but do you think he listens? What is it now? Tell me — I am prepared for the worst."

"He wants to go to Kalavryta."

"Kyrie eleison!" Petro crossed himself. Looking at Stavro, he cried, "Prometheus, have you taken leave of your brains? Kalavryta is another country. We have no relatives there, no friends!"

Kleanthi drew courage from all the commotion and again edged in toward Stavro. Petro lost his patience; he brought up his hand and cuffed the boy sharply on the cheek. "I told you to leave us!" he shouted. But as soon as he had done so his eyes betrayed him — remorse swept over his face. Kleanthi walked away, trembling.

"You did not have to strike him," said Stavro.

"I warned him . . . twice I warned him."

"You are a brave bastard . . . a god-damned brave bastard!"

"Get ready — both of you," yelled Kapetan Thanasi.

"Ready for what?" said Petro.

"We are going to Potami . . . to church."

Petro winced. "Hey, friend Kapetan — I have nothing to confess. God and I are on good terms lately; He goes His way, I go mine. . . ."

"This is the day of the Resurrection," Kapetan Thanasi answered him, solemn-faced.

Petro crossed himself. "In the name of the Father," he said,

70

"have we fallen so soon into Easter? Here in this ill-fated cave I have lost track of everything . . . time, God, everything!"

"Get yourselves ready," said Kapetan Thanasi. He left them and went to tell the others. As soon as he was gone Petro said to Stavro, "Now, what is all this about Kalavryta?"

"Go to hell!"

"In the name of the Virgin, are you still thinking about that little goat? Look, I am sorry — I did not mean to strike him. . . ."

Stavro walked to his cot. He put on his jacket and black forage cap. The others were ready. Kleanthi stood beside the mouth of the cave, waiting — his face still downcast. Panago had just finished his coffee and was reaching down for his bandolier. Kapetan Thanasi saw him and yelled out, "No weapons!"

"What?" Panago snapped back.

"We are going to church — there is no need for guns."

"It is a long journey to Potami," Panago sneered. He did not give Kapetan Thanasi a chance to interrupt him. "Perhaps you are hoping the Germans will be in church also?"

"I have no time to jabber with you, Panago," said Kapetan Thanasi. He shoved on his cap and started out of the cave. All this time Petro did not say one word. When he got outside he placed himself beside Stavro and said, "Why do you want to go to Kalavryta?"

They walked along together. Glaring at the purple peaks above him, Stavro said, "I am going after Pappa Lambro."

"He still has life?"

"I do not know . . . I must find out."

"You do not know? How did you hear about him?"

Stavro told him.

"I shall come with you!" Petro exclaimed.

Stavro did not answer him. They made their way through a rock-ribbed valley flanked on both sides by towers of stone — huge spikes nailed to the sky in endless rows like Neolithic columns. Although Stavro had taken this path once before, when they went to cut the wires, it looked strange and new to him now. Close at his heels he could hear his uncle breathing hard, struggling to keep pace with him. When at last Kapetan Thanasi ordered them to stop and rest beside a small stream, Petro wiped the sweat from his face with the back of his wrist and cried, "Where are we . . . is this Greece? In the name of the Father, I am dying of thirst!" Bracing himself firmly on two stones, he leaned over and shoved his mouth into the water. Quickly, he brought it up again, his lips purple. "Aman," he yelled, "it is like ice!"

Stavro was not thirsty. He sat on a rock beside a lone carob tree and intently followed the course the stream was taking — an obscure handful of water, yet it knew precisely where to go. Born of melting mountain snows, it had only one purpose in life — to reach the valley below in time to feed the new grass, the olive trees, the flowers. . . .

"What are you thinking about, Prometheus?"

"Nothing," said Stavro.

"Whenever I ask you a question, it is always nothing . . . nothing! Admit it — you had your mind on the Cretan."

"I do not know what you are trying to say."

"Pappa Lambro's niece! I am not blind, Prometheus — I have had my eye on you . . . yes, all those '*walks*' you took this winter. You had a good taste of that girl and now you are still hungry — it is written on your face!"

Blind with fury, Stavro could only say, "Go to hell!"

"Not I," yelled Petro. "It is you who shall go to hell . . . you and that ill-fated orphan . . . Is this what drives you to Kala-vryta? Do you think for one minute that such madness can erase your sin? God is not blind, Prometheus!"

His blood raging with turbulence, Stavro had not realized the others had already moved out. Although he really was not thirsty he bent over the stream and took a quick drink; then wiping his mouth nervously he ran after them, leaving his uncle white-faced under the carob tree.

72

2

It was unlike other Resurrections — only a few musket shots into the air, the tiny candles inside the church burning listlessly below the sad-faced icons; hollow cries from the bowels of hunger: *"Christ is Risen! He is truly Risen!"* Stavro's mind sagged under a heavy burden as he walked slowly from the church that night . . . *a Man is born, He suffers, He dies . . . without joy, without tears . . . Alpha and Omega. It is as simple as that . . . .*

Above him the sky glorified itself with millions of bright stars; the moon was abundantly full. A few villagers, protecting their burning candles, proceeded cautiously to their homes. Behind them their children attempted to do the same thing. Stavro remembered his own joy when he brought the Easter candle into his house. It was a good sign, his mother always said, God's resurrected light burning in their house, on their little icon shelf. Stavro never understood what it meant then. He was very young and thought perhaps God had decided to come to their house and live . . . God under Stavro's own roof, sleeping with him, eating with him, living and dying with him . . . but after Stellio died Stavro turned his back on God forever . . . Stellio, who had always symbolized life to him — young, beautiful, radiant life . . . red cheeks, vibrant brown eyes, strong chin, sturdy legs . . . Trismegistos Hermes!

Yes, Stavro buried God with Stellio that day.

They all went to the priest's house to eat. Pappa Thoma, the same number of wrinkles on his bony face, the same gray beard . . . ageless. His wife, Demetroula, a small woman, dark-faced and very thin, bounced from the kitchen to the front room, getting the table ready. She seemed overjoyed to have so many guests in her house. The priest's blessing was brief, for he looked wan and tired after forty days of fasting. They pounced upon the soup even before he had finished. Suddenly Pappa

Thoma stared at his wife as though in great pain. "The wine, Demetroula," he cried. "We forgot the wine!"

She hurried downstairs and came back holding an earthen jug in her hands. Petro took it away from her and started filling the glasses. It was white wine. Pappa Thoma lifted his glass high. "A Good Resurrection!" he cried.

"Christ is Risen!" shouted Kapetan Thanasi with great exuberance.

In a very subdued voice the priest's wife lifted her glass also and said, ". . . and freedom this year."

"Amen," replied Pappa Thoma solemnly.

After a few glasses, Petro unloosened his tongue. Glancing at the priest, he said, "Pappa, now that our stomachs have been properly cared for, thanks to your wife's busy hands, should we not feed our souls as well?"

"Of course," gleamed the priest.

"You will not object if I sing the 'Christ is Risen'?"

"God forbid."

"It is not Easter for me unless I sing the 'Christ is Risen. . . .' "

"Begin . . . begin," cried Pappa Thoma.

Petro stood up. He cleared his throat twice and started in: *'Christ is Risen from the dead, destroying death through His own death, and granting eternal life, even to those in the graves. . . .'* "

They all joined in, filling the priest's house with their thunderous voices. Stavro found himself singing also — words from a buried past, like Christ Himself resurrected . . . ashes unto ashes, earth-eaten, still suffocating from the smell of the grave, sick like the scent of stale flowers . . . .

Petro was bursting with joy. "Hey, Pappa," he cried out, "my soul is still hungry!"

The priest smoothed down his beard carefully and nodded. "Then sing it again . . . sing it again."

"No," said Petro. "It craves something else . . . a tale or two to make us cry or laugh or think of better days."

Pappa Thoma shrugged. "The only stories I know are in the Bible."

Petro frowned. "No, Pappa — we have had enough of Holy Scripture for one night."

"One day in Kalamata," Kleanthi exclaimed, "I saw the king. He came by train and was wearing his white uniform . . ."

"Who asked you to open your mouth, little goat?"

"Let the boy speak," said Kapetan Thanasi. The priest too nodded his head approvingly. But Petro scowled. "And who is the king? Is he some kind of god, a touch-me-not? Little goat, I wish I had been in Kalamata that day — I would have put your king in his place, white uniform and all."

"I take it you are not a royalist," said Pappa Thoma, squinting hard at Petro.

"You have taken it correctly, Pappa."

"Strange, but I thought everyone in these parts loved the king."

"I have my own mind, my own convictions — I do not follow the herd, Pappa."

"You are to be praised," said the priest. His wife got up and cleared the table. She did not wash the dishes — she left them piled up in the sink. Returning to the front room she wished them all a Good Resurrection and went upstairs to bed. Petro drew new courage. "Now that your wife is gone," he said to the priest, "I have something further to tell you about the king — begging your pardon, of course. . . ."

"Proceed, proceed," said Pappa Thoma, showing aggravation at this point. Panago filled the glasses; Stavro lit a cigarette.

"Yes, Pappa," Petro went on, "if I had been in Kalamata that day, I would have said to that touch-me-not: *Friend king, tell me — when do you find it most convenient to move your bowels?*"

Panago dropped his glass and let out a roaring laugh. But Petro silenced him and rushed on, "No doubt my remark might have embarrassed him, but I would have kept at him: *Friend king, enough of this formality — answer me plainly, when do you shit . . . in the morning after breakfast . . . or maybe at night before bed . . . you do shit, do you not? And how about that other matter, friend king — I mean your bladder. Is it in good condition? I had an uncle, Stamati was his name, he had to urinate every ten minutes . . . no matter where he was, what he was doing, Stamati had his hand on his fly . . . I hope you do not have his problem, friend king. . . ."*

"Must we talk about pissing and shitting on the night of the Resurrection?" Panago cried out in a groggy voice.

"And why not, friend Panago? I ask you — who among men has been spared from these natural functions? No one . . . not even Christ!"

The priest straightened up abruptly. "Enough," he warned. But Petro was on fire. "This is one fault I find with Holy Scripture, Pappa — not once does it say if that poor ill-fated Christ paused along the road, or stepped behind a bush. . . ."

"Enough! Enough!"

Petro did not press the point any further. He drained his glass and waited for Panago to fill it again. Pappa Thoma struggled to his feet. He blessed them all hastily and said, "It is not a cold night — some of you can huddle around the jaki, the others are welcome to lie down on the rug in the front room . . . I am sorry but we do not have enough beds for all of you."

Kapetan Thanasi also got up. "Do not trouble yourself," he told the priest. "Your warm house is luxury enough. A light sleep, your Grace, and sweet dreams."

"A Good Resurrection," the priest corrected him. He stopped at the foot of the stairs to bless them once more. Slowly he started up. Before he got to the top step, Petro leaned back and started singing again, *'Christ is Risen from the dead, destroying death through His own death, and granting eternal life, even to those in the grave . . . !"*

76

3

At dawn Stavro awoke and found brilliant shafts of Easter sunlight piercing through the window of the priest's kitchen. The church bell was pounding; from a distant yard a cock crew. Soon the air was vibrant with children's voices . . . clean, angelic, happy voices bubbling over with festive anticipation.

The priest's wife was already at the jaki, making coffee. Pappa Thoma was not up yet. Stavro put on his jacket and walked outside. There was not much to Potami — a little white church, a narrow cobbled street, a few shabby houses. Stavro cut across the street, toward the shrieking children playing on the steps of the church. Even from this distance he could see their thin spindly legs, their bloated little bellies, hollow sunken eyes. They saw Stavro and came running toward him but he could not bear the sight of them — turning back to the priest's yard, he hurried quickly into the house.

The priest was in the kitchen, awake and dressed in his robes. He held a cup of coffee in his hand and was taking loud sips from it. When he saw Stavro, he laid the cup on the kitchen table and offered him his hand. However Stavro acted as though he did not see it and he leaned toward the jaki for the coffeepot. He poured himself a cup.

"Christ is Risen!" Pappa Thoma said to him. His voice sounded hurt.

"He is truly Risen," said Stavro, sipping from his cup. The priest stepped to the door and looked outside. His eyes beamed with delight. "There is no greater joy in all the world," he said, "than the Risen Christ."

Stavro nodded his head.

"Did you sleep well, my son?"

"Yes," said Stavro.

"You got up early."

"I heard the church bell . . ." Stavro could still see that

77

starved look on the children's faces. "You have suffered much, here in Potami," he said.

Pappa Thoma stared at him, puzzled. "Only God knows how much we have suffered," he replied, shaking his head pitifully. "Not a day passes that I do not read the service for the dead. We are wasting away, fainting in the street. For the past three weeks dysentery has been running through our village like a wild brush fire. I pray God it does not turn into cholera or typhus. And yet, we should not complain . . . Potami is more fortunate than other villages. We still manage to find a few roots in the hills . . . some herbs and mussels. These have sustained us. . . ."

"Do not the Germans bring you rations?"

Pappa Thoma gave out a squeaky laugh. "Yes, they have come here with their rations, once or twice . . . a bowl of tasteless soup, a few slices of stale bread . . . each time they came here I assembled my people inside the church . . . they waited patiently and with great expectation, all of them carrying broken plates or old tin cans to hold their portion of soup . . . I praise God we have not turned into beasts — at least not yet . . . we were orderly . . . we did not push or run or get panicky when we first saw the food . . . after it was distributed, I gave the blessing and we all ate . . . many licked their plates and cans dry as they filed out of the church . . . I am an old man — my eyes have seen much, but it turns my stomach when a mother bares a sunken, dry breast to her baby . . . !"

Tears filled the old priest's eyes. He stopped to wipe them with the back of his hand, then went on. "We are a beaten people . . . we do not look like Greeks any longer; our eyes do not burn with hatred when we see the Germans enter our village . . . our spirit is broken, *we are hungry, hungry, hungry!*"

Stavro touched him gently on the shoulder. "You must not speak this way, Pappa Thoma." Then quickly changing the subject, he said, "When were you last in Platano?"

Immediately the priest's eyes brightened. "Ah, Platano," he said. "I have not been there since your aunt died. My soul is heavy with guilt — I must go there soon and visit with Pappa Lambro's wife."

Stavro felt his voice shake as he said, "Pappa Thoma, do you think Pappa Lambro is still alive?"

The old priest crossed himself. "I am certain of it!" he cried. "More certain than death itself. . . ."

Stavro helped himself to another cup of coffee. The priest's wife handed him a small plate of dried-up cheese and a few slices of hard bread. He ate everything. Meanwhile Pappa Thoma opened the door again to watch the children. "Now I understand," he murmured, "what Christ meant when he said: *'Unless ye become as little children, ye shall not inherit the kingdom of heaven . . .'* Look at them, the poor little orphans, their stomachs are bloated, their faces are bleached with death — and yet they shout, they play. In the name of the Virgin, why does not Christ show them His mercy?"

The priest's wife handed Pappa Thoma a small plate of cheese but he pushed it away angrily. "All these years you have been with me," he cried, "and you still give me food before the liturgy!"

"You have fasted forty days," she said, shoving the plate before him again. "Christ is Risen. He wants you to eat . . . look at yourself . . . Thoma, you are a dreadful sight, weak and sick!"

"My mouth shall never touch food before a liturgy!" he shouted.

"You are a stubborn old man!"

Pappa Thoma turned to Stavro and said, "I have something to say to your Kapetan when he awakens."

"I will get him up if you wish," said Stavro.

"No, it can wait — let him sleep."

Stavro lit a cigarette. Pappa Thoma opened the kitchen door and ambled out into the yard. Stavro joined him. They sat on a wooden bench beneath a scrawny grapevine. Stavro took a deep puff.

"Is anything troubling you?" the priest asked him.

"No."

"You are very nervous . . . I noticed it last night when we were eating."

"I smoke a great deal. . . ."

"It is not the smoking. I watch your eyes — they never rest."

"I was thinking about Pappa Lambro. . . ."

"Yes?"

"I have made up my mind to go to Kalavryta."

Pappa Thoma crossed himself. "Have you lost your senses?" he cried.

"I cannot rest until I bring him back to Platano . . . to his home," Stavro said.

"Pappa Lambro is in God's hands — he will return to his people when the time is right . . . when God ordains it."

"If I do not go after him, he will die!" Stavro exclaimed.

"And if you do go, *you* will die," the priest warned him.

Stavro put out his cigarette. He walked back into the house. At the kitchen door he looked back and saw that Pappa Thoma had not stirred from the bench — the priest had his head down, shoulders hunched, and seemed to be talking to himself. Stavro went back to him. He sat beside him on the bench and said, "Pappa Thoma, do you really believe that God ordains our lives?"

"Certainly," cried the priest.

"He ordains everything?"

"Everything."

"The war . . . the occupation . . . thousands dying from hunger . . . ?"

"It is all God's will," grunted Pappa Thoma.

"Then He must delight in seeing little children playing on the church steps with bloated bellies and swollen legs. . . ."

"He does not delight in it — He allows it."

"Why?"

"Because it is part of His plan, His divine plan for all of

us . . . not a sparrow falls without God knowing it. His eye is everywhere."

"He is not a God, but a cannibal!" Stavro yelled.

Pappa Thoma crossed himself in fear. "In the name of Christ," he shuddered, "watch your tongue!" He struggled to get to his feet; Stavro went to help him but the old priest pushed him gruffly away and walked back to the house alone.

Stavro waited a few minutes before going in himself. Kapetan Thanasi was awake and talking in whispers with the priest in the kitchen. Panago was drinking coffee; his uncle also. The others were just then getting up. When Pappa Thoma saw Stavro he scowled and drew Kapetan Thanasi into the front room. Kleanthi touched Stavro on the arm. "What is wrong?" he said. "Why is the priest talking to Kapetan Thanasi?"

"I do not know," said Stavro.

Panago, who had overheard them, said, "Whenever the Kapetan sees a goatbeard he has communion on his mind. . . ."

"Now?" said Kleanthi, making a face.

"Now and forever, Amen!" Panago sneered.

Petro finished with his coffee and came beside them. He had a contrite look on his face. He pulled Stavro to the side and whispered to him, "Forgive me — I did not mean what I said the other day. They were cruel words . . . horrible words. Please say that you forgive me, Stavro. . . ."

Stavro forced a smile.

"You are not angry with me?"

"Forget it," said Stavro.

Petro slapped him fondly on the back. He said, "This is why I have always loved you, Stavro — you are good inside . . . yes, good!"

Panago went to the jaki for a second cup of coffee. When he returned, Kleanthi asked him, "Do you think Kapetan Thanasi will make us take communion again?"

"Little goat," Petro cut in, "it is not such a great problem."

Kapetan Thanasi and the priest came back into the kitchen.

81

In an austere voice the Kapetan said to Stavro, "I must talk with you and your uncle, privately." He led them into the front room and made them sit on the sofa before beginning. "I am afraid I have something unpleasant to say to both of you. . . ."

Here Petro interrupted him. "Speak, friend Kapetan — what can you say to hurt us? My nephew and I have suffered much in this life . . . he has only his mother, and I . . . I have no one. Speak!"

"There is a man in your village who must be killed."

"What?" cried Petro.

"He must be killed immediately."

"Why, friend Kapetan?"

"Because he is a traitor . . . a profiteer!"

"In Platano . . . in my little village? Never!"

"Who is this man?" said Stavro.

"His name is Spero . . . he runs a coffeehouse."

Petro swept into a hysterical laugh. "Barba Spero? He has never harmed a soul. Who told you this lie, friend Kapetan . . . who bears witness against Barba Spero?"

Suddenly Pappa Thoma was in the room. He raised both hands high to silence Petro. "I told the Kapetan!" he exclaimed.

"You are the Judas?" Petro ranted.

Unafraid, the priest looked at him and said, "The truth had to be revealed. This man was seen going into the mountains and coming back with bushels of potatoes. He sold them at exorbitant prices . . . five gold sovereigns a peck!"

"I do not believe it," said Petro. He looked at Stavro as if hoping he too would say something but Stavro only dropped his eyes.

"Speak up!" Petro suddenly yelled out. "Tell Kapetan Thanasi all this is a lie . . . tell him!"

"If Barba Spero was seen," blurted Stavro, "there is nothing to be said."

"Stavro, look me in the eye and tell me that Barba Spero could be guilty of such a crime . . . can you tell me?"

"He was seen," said Stavro.

Petro's face got distorted with anger. "What kind of a bastard are you?" he bellowed. "You have known Barba Spero all your life — has he ever hurt you? Did he ever speak one word against anyone? And you there, Pappa, that day when you came to bury my wife, did I not leave my house to bring you a bottle of wine? Where do you think it came from? *'Take it,'* Barba Spero said to me, *'take it and give it to the priest.'* When I went to pay him he pushed me out of his coffeehouse as if I had insulted him. This is the man you are crucifying, Pappa!"

"He was seen," cried Pappa Thoma, glancing at Kapetan Thanasi for help.

"Who saw him?" yelled Petro.

"Many eyes . . . people in your own village," said the priest. His hands began to shake — he was white-faced.

Kapetan Thanasi came to the priest's aid. "Pappa Thoma has already given me their names. I cannot reveal their identities, but they are trusted people of your village. As I said, this is a very unpleasant task. . . ."

"Friend Kapetan, every coin has two faces. How can you kill a man without first hearing his side of the story?"

"When more than half a dozen people in one small village point their finger no further proof is needed. He is guilty and must die," Kapetan Thanasi shouted.

Petro sobbed, "In the name of the Father, we have become worse than the Germans. If you allow this, friend Kapetan, brothers will betray brothers, and mothers their own children. There will be no end to it."

"Evil must be cut off at the roots," Kapetan Thanasi exclaimed, unmoved.

"Friend Kapetan, I say this to you: if you kill Barba Spero you will have to reckon with his two brothers. Listen to me — Platano will become a pool of blood before this mess is finished. I give you fair warning!" Once more he glared at Stavro but Stavro could not speak. A thick sourness had found his stomach and mouth; his head began pounding.

Kapetan Thanasi cleared his throat for the final time and said,

83

"I shall ask Panago to come with you. I am not concerned who does the killing, or how . . . but I want it done!"

"Three palikars to murder one feeble old man," Petro scowled bitterly.

"It must be done." Kapetan Thanasi could say nothing else but this. He turned and left them. Stavro felt his uncle's probing eyes. He wanted to say something to him but the words got blocked in his throat. Neither could he move.

"Is this what you learned in Athens?" Petro's voice was coarse, disgusted.

"But Uncle Petro . . . he was seen by many eyes. . . . "

"I do not care about the many eyes. I only want to hear what you have to say . . . you, my nephew . . . the son of my dead brother!"

Stavro had to fight with himself to say it: "I cannot go against Kapetan Thanasi. He has commanded us and we must do as he says."

"Not we, Prometheus . . . you! You and that butcher, Panago. . . ."

"Are you not coming with us?"

"I wash my hands," Petro roared. He grabbed Stavro by the arms and held him with great strength. His voice shook, "I have this to say to you — if you lift one finger to harm old Barba Spero, I swear . . . on your grandmother's soul, I swear I will kill you!"

4

In the middle of the night Petro woke Stavro up to tell him that he had changed his mind and was coming with them to Platano. They set out at sunrise with bandoliers and rifles. Kapetan Thanasi came with them as far as the gorge. "I will tell you for the last time," he said emphatically. "This man Spero must be killed . . . do you understand?"

Panago nodded; Stavro said nothing. Petro gave an angry

kick with his foot and sent a stone flying. Kapetan Thanasi frowned. "I do not want any trouble from you!"

Petro pleaded with him, "Friend Kapetan — for the good of your soul . . . spare Barba Spero . . . I implore you."

"He must be killed," Kapetan Thanasi barked.

"Come, we are wasting time," Panago said.

"Butcher, shut your mouth!" Petro yelled, raising his hand. Kapetan Thanasi quickly stepped between them. "None of this," he warned. "You have a job to do . . . the sooner it is done, the better. Now then, do your crosses. Go to the Good . . . !"

Petro laughed cynically. Kapetan Thanasi said to him again, "I want no trouble from you!"

"I hear you, friend Kapetan . . . I hear you. Three Kyrie eleisons and *pftt* . . . it is a simple matter. God protect us."

"Come," cried Panago again.

Petro lost his patience. "Butcher, I sleep with your mother . . . I sleep with your grandmother, and with all your ugly ancestors!"

"Go to hell!" Panago bellowed.

They started out. Kapetan Thanasi turned and headed back for the cave. Stavro smoked a full cigarette before Petro finally spoke. They had come face-to-face with a glistening wall of rock and stopped to catch their breath. Petro said to Panago, "I am sorry I called you butcher."

Panago measured him, scowling.

". . . also for what I said about your mother, your grandmother, and all your ugly ancestors. . . ."

Still Panago did not answer him. Petro slapped him on the shoulder. "I am talking to you."

"I hear you."

"Why do you not speak? I said I was sorry."

Panago squinted at the sun.

"What are you looking at?" said Petro.

"I am wondering what time it is."

"Why?"

"We do not want to be late getting into Platano."

Petro flared up. "You cannot wait to get your hands on that ill-fated man!" Panago's reply was a tight grip over his rifle. Petro looked at Stavro. "Your butcher friend is counting the seconds," he said. "Tick-tock, tick-tock . . . he cannot hold his breath until he has his piece of meat and glass of blood. Do not think for one minute, nephew, that the Great Clockmaker is not following us today . . . mark my words — His eye has not closed from the time we left the cave."

Panago heard him and said, "What Clockmaker?"

"The Eternal Clockmaker!"

"I do not understand what you are trying to say, Barba. . . ."

Petro grabbed him by the collar of his jacket. "I warned you once before!" he cried.

"Warned me about what?"

"That name . . . *Barba*. Where I come from it means old man."

"It means the same thing where I come from," Panago replied. He was wearing a defiant grin.

Petro shrugged. "It is hopeless arguing with you — your soul, friend Panago, is choked with too many weeds. Apparently you have your heart set on going through life ignorant." Panago tried to say something to him but Petro pushed on, "When I used the term *Clockmaker* I spoke for your benefit — this is a trick Christ Himself often employed. He never came out with things. He had to use riddles and parables because the world was in a pitiful state . . . illiterate, ignorant, worshipping money, food, and women. Sodom and Gomorrah, if you follow me, friend Panago."

"I follow you."

"If I had said *God* instead of *Clockmaker,* perhaps you would have made a face and paid no attention to me. But, you see, I spoke to your ignorance. . . ."

"Get on with it," Panago told him.

". . . behind every parable lies a moral. . . ."

"God damn you, get on with it!"

"Slowly, friend Panago. Slowly. There is no short path to God's kingdom. You have to suffer many lumps on your head, and the weeds in your soul must be plucked out one at a time. . . . Listen to me — in the very beginning of all things, there was no earth, sun, stars, moon, or sky. No, only the Great Clockmaker. . . ."

"Then you *are* speaking of God?"

"Who else? But you must understand one thing — He was not always a Clockmaker. In the beginning He was a Do-Nothing. He refused to work with His hands and, as a result, He suffered severe periods of depression and melancholy. One day He made up His mind — He would start using His hands. . . . He put together a small clock, being very careful to make it into His exact image . . . round face, short stubby hands, a strong steady beat . . . if you follow me, friend Panago. . . ."

"Amen, Amen — I follow you!"

". . . After He had finished with it, He wound it up until it started ticking on its own. But the poor ill-fated thing was very unhappy — it had no companions, no one to share its joys. So the Great Clockmaker, feeling sorry for it, quickly went about making another clock. He took a wheel or two, plus a few odds and ends from the first clock, and in a matter of minutes He had created a second clock. Ah, friend Panago — this was truly paradise . . . two little clocks ticking away at each other in perfect rythmn and ecstasy. . . ."

"Go on," said Panago.

". . . He was so pleased with His work, this Great Clockmaker, He decided to make a whole universe of clocks . . . all sizes and colors; all shapes."

Suddenly Panago interrupted him. "Stop . . . you are filling my ears with nonsense!"

"Why do you say that, friend Panago?"

"I am not your friend. I can see through you now — you are trying to take my mind away from what we have to do."

Petro scowled back at him. "You and my nephew here have already made up your minds about Barba Spero. What can I do to sway you now?"

"I do not believe you," said Panago.

"I swear it," Petro cried.

"Why did you change your mind and come with us?"

"Did not Kapetan Thanasi command me to come?"

"You refused . . . at first you refused. *'I wash my hands . . .'* This is what you said."

"Yes — but I am here, am I not?"

"I do not trust you!" Panago roared. He looked toward Stavro as though he wanted him to say something also but Stavro took out another cigarette and lit it. Petro flung up his hands. "Friend Panago," he said, "you are trying my patience. How can I possibly prevent you from killing Barba Spero?"

"With your sweet talk, and your fables."

"I do not speak in fables, friend Panago — I am trying to reach you as Christ reached the multitudes . . . in parable. You have ears; open them. How long must you walk in darkness? Have you no concern for your soul's future?"

Again, Panago looked at Stavro. "Can you not stop him?" he yelled.

"Let him talk," said Stavro.

"He bothers me!"

"Block your ears . . . do not listen to him," said Stavro. He walked past them and took the lead. The terrain was more familiar to him now — they were approaching the shadows of Platano. Another mound of small hills and they would be there. In his mind he rehearsed everything once more: he could clearly see the fearful look in Barba Spero's eyes, see his aged hands shake, his whole body tremble . . . he could hear the old man's sobs, trace the tears down his wrinkled face, feel the groaning anguish of his heart . . .

And who, thought Stavro, who shall pull the trigger?

Petro's voice broke the silence. "We have not far to go, friend Panago — may I finish what I started to say?"

"Finish," Panago barked.

"We were speaking of clocks . . . yes, a whole universe of clocks, tick-tocking, making a horrible racket, in fact creating so much confusion and bedlam the Great Clockmaker is forced to cover up His ears and scream. And in this moment of agony, friend Panago, He is so sorry for having created all these noisy clocks, He lifts up His fist and is about to bring it down and destroy them all, when suddenly the clock He loved the most, a little white thing with a sad face and thin arms, beseeches Him not to do it. . . ."

"Christ," Panago exclaimed.

"Of course, Christ," Petro replied. "He is the little white clock with the sad face and thin arms. He promises the Great Clockmaker he will personally bring peace and quiet among the noisy clocks, and those making the loudest racket he will destroy by hurling them into the eternal flames, never to tick again."

"I think I am beginning to see your point," Panago said. "Is this how Christ always spoke?"

"Always," said Petro. "Shall I continue?"

"Continue."

"As you can now guess, the little white clock managed to quiet down the noisy clocks — but mind you, only for a short time. As soon as he turned his face to leave them, however, they started in again, making even a louder racket than before. . . ." Petro stopped here for a long moment, deep in thought.

"Well, get on with it!" growled Panago. "What happened next?"

"Nothing, friend Panago. Nothing happened that is not happening this very minute. Open your ears and listen . . . can you not hear all these noisy clocks still banging away at each other . . . Italians, Germans, and now you and Prometheus here? Heaven help us — the Great Clockmaker will surely bang His fist down upon us all if you murder Barba Spero!"

"You are full of goatshit!" Panago yelled, furious.

"Tick-tock, tick-tock . . ."

89

"God damn it, you are full of goatshit up to your ears!"

Fearlessly, Petro pushed Panago aside and got behind Stavro. They reached the last hill. Below them lay Platano, sparkling white in the noon sun. They saw the sea — it looked drowsy, as though it were about to prepare itself for a nap. Although they were still one full kilometer from Barba Spero's coffee-house, Stavro could feel Anna in his arms — smell her skin and hair. But then he thought of Barba Spero and shuddered. Every downhill step he took flooded his heart with pain. Along with this, his uncle's jabbering voice would not stop: "Tick-tock, tick-tock . . ."

5

Barba Spero sat with two old men at a table near the window. The door of his coffeehouse was wide open, allowing a mild breeze from the sea to sweep in unmolested. When he saw Petro the old man pushed back his chair and ran to embrace him. Tears streamed down his face. "Petro," he cried, "it is you . . . really you?"

"Yes, friend Barba, it is I." Petro too was overcome. He clamped both arms around Barba Spero in a viselike grip and kissed him on the cheek. "I am home again," he said. "I am home!"

"Sit down," said Barba Spero, turning to the others. "I will get you some coffee."

Panago, however, threw up his hands and stopped him. "We did not come here for a social visit, Barba," he said. But Petro broke in on him. "Bring the coffee, Barba — we have plenty of time," he yelled.

With a troubled look on his face Barba Spero went to get the coffees. After he laid them down on an empty table he braced his hands against the back of a chair for a moment, then sat down. The two old men at the adjoining table, sensing perhaps that something was wrong, picked up their caps and hobbled out of the coffeehouse. Panago did not waste any time. He pointed his finger at Barba Spero. "You are a traitor!" he bellowed.

Barba Spero's face grew pale; he made a desperate effort to get to his feet but Panago gruffly pushed him back. He motioned to Petro. "Stay by the door . . . allow no one inside!"

Petro retreated a few paces toward the door. "I warn you," he said, "do not harm Barba Spero — he is my friend!"

"Close your mouth and stand by the door," Panago ordered him. Turning to Stavro, he said, "Keep your eye on your uncle — I do not trust him. If he makes one false move I will kill him."

"I sleep with your mother!" Petro yelled from the door. Panago paid no attention to him. He grabbed a chair, slid it beside Barba Spero and sat down. Stavro could feel his own blood boiling. He wanted to wipe the ugly smirk from Panago's face but somehow felt powerless. He stood there, looking out the window toward the square. It was empty and quiet. A huge black shadow lay sprawled like an ink blot beneath the plane tree. Without Pappa Lambro the church looked deserted and Godforsaken. It reminded Stavro of a lullaby his mother often sang to him . . . words that saddened him even as a small boy:

> *High, high in the mountain*
> *stands an abandoned church,*
> *it has no one to ring its semantron . . .*
> *no chanter . . .*
> *no priest!*

Panago's voice shattered the silence. "Admit it, Barba," he shouted. "You are a traitor to your country!"

"No," cried Barba Spero. "I have done nothing wrong . . . nothing. . . ." His sobs were like a knife in Stavro's heart.

"Do you deny selling potatoes for gold sovereigns?"

"I did not ask for the sovereigns — they forced me to take them . . . I am not a traitor!"

"Five gold sovereigns for one peck of potatoes?"

"Three, five, I do not remember," choked Barba Spero. "They shoved them into my hands and grabbed the potatoes . . . they were like animals . . . !"

"Nevertheless, you kept the sovereigns?"

"Yes."

"You are a profiteer!"

"No, no . . ." Barba Spero whimpered. He pointed to an old oak desk against the rear wall of the coffeehouse, "The sovereigns are all there," he exclaimed, "inside the middle drawer. Go, see for yourself. They do me no good . . . what can I buy with them — meat, clothing, wine . . . ?"

Panago did not move.

". . . The sovereigns shall stay there until the last German leaves Greece," Barba Spero sobbed. "I have kept an accurate record . . . each one of them is accounted for. I am not a traitor!"

"There, you see?" yelled Petro. "Barba Spero is innocent."

"Shut your mouth," Panago barked. Turning he pounced on Barba Spero again. "Why did you go into the mountains in the first place?"

"My cousin Theophilos lives there — he has a farm. When I went to see him he was overjoyed. He tied two sacks of potatoes to his donkey and told me to distribute them equally among the distressed in the village, but when I returned home they fell on me like dogs. I could not hold them back. . . ."

"How many times did you go to your cousin's farm?"

"Only once . . . I am an old man and it is a very long climb."

"You went to make money — admit it!"

"No."

"Then why?"

In a burst of tears Barba Spero blurted out, "We lost the war . . . must we now perish? I did what little I could to keep my village alive. . . ."

"You did not have to take the money," Panago roared. He made a grab for his rifle. Barba Spero clasped his hands together and moaned, "No, no!"

Stavro could bear to hear no more. Spinning angrily around, he said to Panago, "Leave him alone . . . he is an old man."

"Keep out of this," Panago warned him. Stavro tried to pull the rifle away from Panago but with a wild cry Panago clenched his fist and struck him on the face, knocking him to the floor. Dazed, Stavro saw Panago aim the rifle at Barba Spero. He made a frantic effort to get up, but the blast deafened him. He heard his uncle cry out, "Stavro . . . Stavro!"

Panago was slumped on the floor, blood gushing from his mouth. His body twitched and rolled like a hen that had just lost its head. Barba Spero started weeping hysterically. Petro looked stunned. His rifle hung loosely in his hands as though it were stuck there and he could not release it from his fingers.

"In the name of the Father," he moaned. "What have I done . . . what have I done?"

Stavro came and leaned over Panago. He was dead. Barba Spero crossed himself and buried his head in both hands, sobbing like a frightened child. Stavro said to both of them, "Help me get him out of here."

Together, they dragged Panago outside and crossed the street into the churchyard. A shovel was leaning against the cellar door of the church. Stavro took it and handed it to his uncle. Petro was still white-faced. Stavro then grabbed Panago under the armpits and dragged him into the cemetery, stopping at a place where he could see no graves. He dug the hole himself while Petro stood behind him, trembling and talking to himself. After he rolled Panago into the hole Petro rushed toward him and clutched him by the legs. "Help me, Stavro!" he cried.

Stavro made him get up. He covered the grave quickly then took hold of Petro's arm. In a stiff voice he said to him, "Come."

"Stavro, I am afraid. . . ."

"Come."

"We cannot return to the cave . . . Kapetan Thanasi will kill me!"

"We are not going back," Stavro said. "I am taking you with me . . . to Kalavryta."

FOUR

Dᴇᴄᴇᴍʙᴇʀ!

Winds of winter . . . long nights and freezing rain . . . hunger and death everywhere — in Sparta, in Megalopolis, Tripoli, Dimitsana, Kastania . . . However, Stavro and his uncle pushed onward, slicing their way through endless mountains and across swollen streams until at last they reached the foothills of Aroania, the last sentinels before Kalavryta. Heeding a sudden fear, Stavro decided to bypass the mountain and enter the city from the north.

They found shelter that night in the Monastery of the Great Cave. The monks were seated in the refectory and about to start eating when Stavro and his uncle walked in. The abbot immediately got up and offered them a place at the table. He said his name was Father Eusebios. He was middle-aged, bone-thin. A thick red beard covered his face. He explained between mouthfuls that they had just finished with vespers, after which they chanted the Great Canon to the Virgin. He had a high-pitched, very excitable voice, but there was warmth in it. He showed real alarm when Stavro told him they were going into Kalavryta.

"No," he warned, "you must not go there!"

"Why not?" said Stavro.

"There was trouble near there . . . in Kerpini. A whole company of German grenadiers was annihilated by guerrilla forces . . . already the Germans have struck back — Zachlorou lies in ruins . . . did you not see it with your own eyes?"

"Yes," said Stavro.

"Zachlorou is only the beginning. Listen to me — Kalavryta may be next. Stay here with us a few days longer. You will be safe."

"What if the Germans come?" Petro finally spoke out.

"They will not harm you," said Father Eusebios. Turning quickly to the side, he motioned to one of the monks, then whispered something into his ear. The novice hurried out of the refectory and came back with two black cassocks. Father Eusebios gave one to Petro. "Here," he said, "put this on — it is the armor of Christ. It will be your protection if the Germans do come." He handed the other cassock to Stavro. At first Stavro held back, but the abbot insisted. Petro, on the other hand, needed no urging. He threw the cassock over his shoulders then, turning to Father Eusebios, he said, "Your Grace, when I was a small boy my father teased me. *'Petro,'* he used to say, *'I think I will make you a monk. . . .'*"

The abbot laughed.

"Who knows?" said Petro, smiling. "Perhaps he was right — I may decide to join you some day. . . ."

"You will be most welcome," Father Eusebios replied.

"I am not a young man any longer, Your Grace — I am forty-eight years old."

"Age is no barrier here. Do you see that old monk, there at the far end of the table? He is Brother Antonios," he pointed to a thin, stoop-shouldered man hunched over the table; his white-forked beard was touching his plate of soup. "Brother Antonios is eighty-seven," sighed the abbot. "He came to us a long time ago in the pit of despair . . . his wife had just died."

"I too have lost a wife," Petro said.

"May her memory be eternal," the abbot said, crossing himself. The monks noticed this and did likewise. Although there was still a deep sadness in Petro's eyes he seemed eager to talk. "I am certain God does not want me to be happy," he told the abbot.

"Why do you say that?"

"He is always taking things away from me ... first my sons, then my daughter, and now my wife. ..."

"He whom the Lord loves ... He chastises," said the abbot.

Petro flung up his hands in anguish. "Must God love me so much?" he cried. "Who am I ... I ask you, who am I?"

"God loves us all — it is His nature to love."

"No, not me — He does not love me."

"Of course He does," said Father Eusebios soothingly.

"I am not clean!" Petro yelled. Before the abbot could open his mouth, Petro cried out, "I have killed a man!" He tried to act casual about it but was failing miserably. "I shot him in the back ... *pftt!* Ask my nephew here ... ask him."

"Keep quiet!" said Stavro.

"I am confessing to Father Eusebios. ..."

"I said keep quiet!"

Reluctantly, Petro lowered his head and resumed eating. After a while he said to the abbot, "I had an uncle who could sing the Byzantine chant — his name was Foti. Such a divine voice! I tell you, Your Grace, he could make death die. ..."

"Was he a priest?"

"No."

"A monk, then?"

"God forbid, no. Foti was a simple goatherd like myself. When a man is alone in the hills it is an easy matter to live close to God. Whoever heard Uncle Foti chanting, would say, *'Aman, he is speaking with God ... he is speaking with God!'* "

"It is a pity he never served God. ..."

"He did, Your Grace. He served God with his voice."

"Perhaps you are right," said the abbot in deep thought.

9 7

"There are many ways a man can serve God. He does not have to put on robes or hide in a monastery. . . ."

"You do not speak like other goatbeards," said Petro, scratching his head. "No, not at all."

Father Eusebios turned to Stavro and said, "Are you not married?"

"No."

"How many years do you have?"

"Twenty-three."

"My nephew is a philosopher, Your Grace . . . he has studied in the University, at Athens."

The abbot's eyes lit up. "Is this true?" he asked Stavro.

"I was in Athens when the war broke out. . . ."

"And you studied philosophy?"

"I took a few courses," Stavro said. He was beginning to feel uncomfortable. He picked up his spoon and began eating. The abbot leaned back in his chair and sighed deeply. "I have never been to Athens, but it is my lifelong dream. . . ."

"You have missed nothing," Petro exclaimed.

"I must go there before I die . . . I want to stand in the center of the Acropolis and . . ."

Petro broke in, sneering: "And what is the Acropolis but chunks of marble piled atop each other? I cannot understand this ecstasy over dead things. I visited Athens after the war in 1924 . . . yes, I made the pilgrimage . . . I climbed the marble steps and planted myself under the Parthenon. I tell you I got the most dreadful feeling, as though I were standing in a graveyard. I could not eat or sleep for many days after. . . ."

The abbot smiled. "Nevertheless, I still intend to go there — God willing, of course." He crossed himself and once more the monks saw him and did the same thing. Petro did not say another word. They finished eating and stood up, heads bowed, while Father Eusebios mumbled a soft prayer of thanks. Slowly, they all filed out of the refectory. A stiff wind struck their faces. Shivering, the monks scattered across the quadrangle to their cells. Father Eusebios took Stavro by the arm and led him to the far wall that overlooked Zachlorou. The tiny village seemed deathly quiet and still. Stavro noticed the tears filling the abbot's eyes. Trembling, he said to Stavro, "Only yesterday Zachlorou was full of life and happy, we could hear the children's voices, the church bell, the dogs, the goats . . ."

As he talked Stavro's mind wandered off . . . *Anna, Anna . . . always Anna. There was so much he wanted to say to her . . . but this is the way God moves: He allows you to take a quick look into tomorrow; He sits quietly by while you make plans, prepare the road, but when at last you start out, tomorrow suddenly becomes yesterday, and God is laughing in your face . . . .*

Stavro put his hand on the abbot's shoulder. "Come," he said. "It is getting cold — I am afraid we are in for a storm."

They cut across the quadrangle, toward the cell row. When the abbot reached his door he stopped and looked at Stavro. "I have one consolation," he said, red-eyed. "You and your uncle are in God's bosom here — no harm shall come to you."

"We cannot stay here very long," Stavro said.

"You must, my son! The world burns, can you not see it?"

It started to rain. Father Eusebios opened the door of the cell and nudged Stavro inside. Stavro saw a bed, a narrow window, the door . . . nothing else. The abbot lit the brazier and sat on the edge of his bed rubbing his hands. His eyes were still glazed. "All roads into Kalavryta are sealed," he said. "I implore you — stay here with us until the German cools his head."

Stavro did not want to talk about it further. He started for the door but the abbot would not let him leave. "Tell me," he said, "what is this about your uncle?"

When Stavro did not reply the abbot said, "Did he kill someone . . . actually?"

"Yes."

"Was it a German?"

"No."

"An Italian."

"No."

"Who then?"

"One of our own men," said Stavro.

"In the name of the Father!" cried the abbot.

They both remained silent for a long time. Stavro's eyes were drawn to the soft flames in the brazier. Bitterly, he thought, the world must have been born of fire . . . eternal fire burning its path through the low road of Hades, through earth and water, and high heaven . . . a steady flame in an unstable world of life and death, joy and pain.

The rain was falling hard now, splattering loudly against the cobbled quadrangle. Through the narrow window Stavro saw the sky turning solidly black and ominous . . . a sky that some-how reminded him of Stellio — cold, hard, very still.

"Is it really so important for you to go to Kalavryta?" Father Eusebios asked him.

"Yes."

"To risk your life . . . your uncle's also?"

"Yes . . . yes!"

"Why?"

Stavro told him about Pappa Lambro. The abbot listened intently and after Stavro finished, he said, "Indeed you must love your priest very dearly."

"I do love him," said Stavro. Immediately the cruel words he hurled at Pappa Lambro that day in Petro's house bounced back at him: *"God is where your belly is . . . !"* They were buried so deeply in his soul he would never forget them.

"My son, this is not love . . . it is insane compulsion. You are willingly throwing your life away. Can you not see it?"

"I only know that I must find him — I cannot rest until I do."

The abbot smiled at him. "But there is no need to drive your-self . . . promise you will stay with us a few days."

"No," said Stavro.

The abbot insisted. "Until Monday . . . that is only three days away. Surely you can wait until then . . . ?"

Stavro struggled with himself. "Very well," he said. "But only until Monday."

The abbot touched him on the head with his fingers and blessed him, saying, "Go to the Good. We shall meet again in the morning after matins." He offered his hand for Stavro to kiss but Stavro did not take it.

2

Later, after his uncle had said good night to him and the sounds of the monastery had faded into soft whispers, Stavro lay in his bed, hands behind his head and thought of Anna. His passion for her had become an open wound . . . each night holding her in his arms, kissing her, making love to her . . . it did not bother him that he could do these things — here inside the cell of a monastery, lying on the same bed where a saintly monk perhaps had lain and thought of higher things: visions, heavenly hopes, the second view of life . . . inside this womb of rock surely a monk was reborn; he saw the illusive light, touched the hem of Christ's garment . . . and yet, would God enter into such a place? Would He breathe this rancid air, soil His fingers on these dirty walls? Would God seek out each monk that slept on this bed, touch him on the forehead and say, *"Today thou shalt be with me in paradise . . . ?"*

And this uncle of his — this shadow of a man lying here at his side, filling the cold room with his snores — what should be done with him? What? Should God touch him also and say, *"Petro, rise up and walk! Behold, your house is once again in order . . . your wife lives; your sons and daughter also . . . ."*

But what does it profit him to think of Petro . . . to think of God, or death, or life? He must think only of Anna — see her there in the kitchen of Pappa Lambro's house, as he did that hot summer night when the priest and his wife were at vespers.

He knocked on the door but when no one answered he turned the knob and walked in. Anna was bent over the sink, washing her hair. She did not hear him. She had on a white slip and stood barefoot on the cold floor. He teased his passion, forced it to stare upon her, restraining even his breath so that she would not hear him. He took one step toward her, then threw his arms around her waist — heard her gasp out. He put his lips on her bare neck, her shoulders. She recognized his arms and allowed him to spin her around and clamp his mouth on hers; a long hard kiss. Her lips squirmed against his so much he could not know whether they were frightened or trying to speak. He pressed down upon them even harder, draining her body into his, through his mouth, his hands, his fingers . . . When he felt her struggling he let her go.

"Stavro," she panted.

"Anna."

"How did you get in here?"

"The door was open."

"You must not stay."

"Where is Pappa Lambro?"

"At vespers."

"And your aunt?"

"She also."

He took her into his arms again and said, "Anna, there is no need to fear." But she pulled away from him and quickly brought her hands to her bosom.

"Do you not trust me?" he said.

"It is not that."

"What then?"

"I do not know . . ." she murmured. He touched her hair — caressed it first, then twisted two long ends around his fingers and pulled her in closer. His eyes fell on her heaving bosom. "Anna," he whispered, "I am in love with you."

"Stavro . . ."

"I have loved you from the first moment I saw you."

She lowered her eyes; her cheeks flushed. She placed her hands over her bosom again and said to him in a shaking voice, "I must put on my dress."

He let her hair go, but not before kissing her again — her lips were still moist. He was on fire. He eased both straps of her slip from her shoulders then swept her into his arms. He felt her body stiffen but he would not release her. His hunger turned into great strength — he lifted her in his arms and carried her to the sofa in the front room. Lying there on her back, her hands clasped, her legs tight together, she threw him a frightened look.

"I want you, Anna," he said, dropping to his knees before her.

"No," she whimpered. A tear trickled down her cheek.

"Anna, do not be afraid . . ." He put his hand on her bare thigh — ran it up and down tenderly. Leaning closer, he tugged her slip down with his fingertips; his lips found her bare breast. She shuddered when he kissed it, then hungrily cupped it with her hands, begging him to do it again. . . .

Petro's loud snores startled him. He got up from the bed and started pacing the floor. When the snoring did not stop he reached for his trousers, put them on, and went outside.

The night was alone with itself — bitter cold and sad. The stars appeared to have lost their joy and were sputtering weakly in the sky like candles in a windstorm. Stavro walked across the wet quadrangle, stopping alongside the wall to light a cigarette. He could still smell Zachlorou below him, reeking with death. He had to laugh at himself: he was a ghost here . . . stuffing his ribs with one day's rations . . . one person had he found . . . only one person in this insane lie of breathing and dying . . . someone he could touch, feel her heartbeat, the warmth of her skin against his . . . one living soul in this whole stinking graveyard and she had to be torn from him, one hundred kilometers away . . . .

His uncle's voice stunned him, "Stavro . . . where are you?"

"I am here," he answered, his heart pounding.

Petro came and stood beside him, panting in his face. "I got up to take a piss," he exclaimed. "I saw your empty bed and got frightened. Are you ill?"

"No," said Stavro. He crushed out his cigarette against the wall. "Why were you frightened?"

"Why, he says! Have you not heard the dreadful things that go on in these places? May God protect us . . . monks, monasteries — they are the works of the devil. God wants no part of them. This sort of thing is unnatural — grown men living together, eating together, sleeping together . . . You did not tell me what you are doing out here."

"I could not sleep," said Stavro. He took out another cigarette and lit it.

Petro said, "Prometheus, what is it about you? Everywhere we go, you latch yourself to a goatbeard . . . why?"

"That is not true," said Stavro.

"Is it not? Look back, Prometheus — there is a whole string of them dangling from your tail . . . Pappa Lambro, Pappa Thoma, Pappa Demetrios, and now this abbot. What do you expect to find from them . . . tell me."

"I am not looking for anything."

"Then leave them alone — why do you keep running to them every chance you get?"

Changing the subject, Stavro said, "Father Eusebios does not want us to leave the monastery until Monday. . . ."

"Three more days?"

"Yes."

"I say we leave at sunrise — the quicker the better!"

"Why?" said Stavro.

"Because the fish stinks first from the head, that is why. I do not like this place. The sooner we unbutton ourselves from it, the better."

Stavro's cigarette had spent itself — he tossed it over the wall and lit another. Now, long ribs of gray clouds began moving across the black sky with violent swiftness. The wind changed and suddenly stopped; everything grew still.

"I did not speak the truth a while back," said Petro.

Stavro inhaled deeply and waited for him to go on. "I did not have to piss," said Petro. "That was not why I got up."

"Why then?"

"I had a nightmare . . . it was about Stellio . . ."

"I do not want to hear it," said Stavro, angrily. He turned his back on him and started walking away. Petro came after him. "Stavro, wait!" he cried.

"No."

"It is not what you think, Stavro — please let me tell you."

"No, damn it, no!"

They reached their cell door — it was wide open. After they got in Stavro closed it and lit the brazier. Petro stood by the bed watching him.

"Go to sleep," said Stavro.

"I cannot close my eyes until I tell you, Stavro . . . your father came to me and said, '*Brother Petro, tell Stavro — tell him how his little brother died —*' "

"I told you I do not want to hear it!"

"— He was with three other boys. They had just come into the village, looking for food . . . they saw the German soldiers rolling a cart through the street — there was a dead donkey on it . . . they followed the Germans into the hills, saw them bury the ill-fated thing, and after the Germans left, Stellio and the three boys dug it up and roasted it over a fire . . . when it came time to eat, the others would not touch it because it had a foul smell . . . but Stellio ate . . . yes, he ate . . ."

"Is this what you had to tell me?"

"Yes. . . ."

Stavro took off his jacket and climbed into bed. Petro did the same thing. Once under the blankets, he said to Stavro, "I feel better now — it has passed."

"You have said enough — go to sleep!"

After a short silence Petro said, "It is a shame you never got to know your father, Stavro — I mean, really know him . . . he was a giant of a man . . . a tall oak, the most handsome palikar in Platano. The girls flocked around him like flies on a donkey's back, but his eyes fell on your mother . . . yes, only on Marika. . . ."

Stavro put his hands behind his head and leaned back, listening to every word. He had a vivid picture of his father: he remembered most the callused hands, his inordinate love for earth and olive trees, the eternal pride of doing the same thing his father had done before him, and his grandfather, and his great-grandfather . . . but Stavro wanted no part of this sickening pastoral succession. Even as a boy he fought against it. *"You are a dreamer!"* his father thundered at him whenever Stavro tried to talk to him about Athens and the new life that was waiting for him there. *"You are born of the earth and you shall die in it!"* Before the burning anger of his words could blow cold, the Italians had invaded Greece and Stavro's father lay lifeless on a hill near Koritsa.

But not so Stellio. Even before he was old enough to make such a decision he promised himself to the land. He would have kept his word were it not for that vile morsel of donkey meat still eating away at his stagnant insides.

Petro rubbed his chin several times and said, "I meant to ask God a special favor this Easter but it left my mind completely. I wanted to say to Him, *'Friend God, soon it will be time for You to soil Your hands once again. Yes, You will have to take that dreadful journey below and dig out Your Son, shake Him back to life again . . . would it be too much to ask You, friend God, if You could also dig out my Zacharo . . . I mean, as long as Your hands will be soiled digging out Your Son . . . and listen, friend God, right beside her are my three children . . . and my brother, Costa . . . and his son, Stellio. . . .'"*

"Close your mouth and go to sleep!" Stavro cried.

106

"Kyrie eleison . . ." mumbled Petro. He rolled over to his side, hunching the blankets snugly over his shoulders.

He did not say good night to Stavro.

3

After matins on Monday morning Stavro and his uncle walked into the refectory with Father Eusebios and the monks for their last meal together. In a way Stavro hated to leave. He had found something at the monastery — he could not be certain what it was. He knew only that he felt a lightness of heart, an exhilarating sense of tranquility and peace. Perhaps it was because he had made up his mind about Kalavryta . . . He recalled what his uncle said back in the cave: *"Strange, but death is never as we dread it to be . . ."* It must be so with Kalavryta. It must be that it does not take much for a man to be a man . . . he has only to look ahead, never to the side, or back. . . .

As soon as they finished eating Father Eusebios took Stavro by the arm and said to him, "Before you leave, walk with me for a few minutes into the hills."

"It is late."

"I shall not keep you . . . come." The abbot led him out of the quadrangle gate, into the high rocks beyond the monastery. The air was warm; the sky clear. Below them Zachlorou appeared to have thrown off her sackcloth of mourning and was trying hard to smile in the brilliant sunlight. They reached the crest of a steep cliff and stopped beside a wide slab of graystone. Stavro sat down and lit a cigarette.

"Tell me," said Father Eusebios, still standing, "what will you do after the war?"

"I do not know," said Stavro.

"Are you not going back to Athens?"

"Perhaps . . . I am not certain."

"I have the feeling you will never be happy unless you do return there."

"Happiness can never be found!" Stavro exclaimed.

"You speak foolishly," said Father Eusebios. "God put us here so that we may be happy."

"And who is God?"

"He is the beginning, and the end . . . without Him we cannot move nor have our being."

"Nor can He move or have His being without us!"

Father Eusebios remained calm. Smiling, he said, "No man can be truly happy unless he believes in God. Life would be entirely meaningless for me if God had not entered my soul. His presence enriches me. I know He exists because I can feel Him here, inside me, breathing new life into my lungs."

"Does He have a sad face?" said Stavro.

"Yes . . . how can He rejoice when the world suffers?"

". . . And does He have a white beard, a kind mouth?"

The abbot laughed. "Some see Him that way, others see Him as a pure spirit. I can say only this — my love for Christ is a spiritual thing . . . it transcends the eye and ear. . . ."

"Perhaps our ancestors were wrong," Stavro said.

"What do you mean?"

" . . . Perhaps there was no glory in Greece. . . ."

"Do you want us to go back . . . back to the gods of Olympus . . . to those myths and fables?"

"Yes."

"I cannot believe in a god who made love to women," said Father Eusebios, grinning, ". . . a god who fought with other gods, who cursed, lied, and even murdered."

"And yet, you find it easy to believe in a god who walked on the sea, who changed water into wine, flew into the air like a bird, and with a snap of his fingers was able to feed five thousand people . . . ?"

Father Eusebios' face grew tight. "Come," he said, "we had better start back."

"I was afraid I would make you angry," Stavro said.

The abbot smiled stiffly. "I am not angry," he said. "I am

frightened for you — you cannot go through life feeling this way, harboring such thoughts. And what of Christ . . . His birth, His agony and death, His resurrection . . . are these nothing but lies?"

"Christ was born," said Stavro, " . . . He suffered, and He died. It ends there."

"And the resurrection?"

"No man has overcome death," Stavro cried. "No man." Suffocating with bitterness, he spun around and looked straight into the abbot's eyes. "A new god reigns in Greece today," he said. "A self-created god of signs and wonders, one hand watching the other — a god of *evil eyes,* icons, threats of everlasting punishment. I cannot believe in this kind of god . . . I cannot nurse my soul on the milk of a fleshless logos . . . !"

Father Eusebios walked slowly away from him. When he came to the very edge of the cliff he looked down. Stavro moved up behind him. He had not realized they had climbed to such a great height. Hundreds of feet below them lay nests of boulders squashed together like tiny agates in a boy's palm. Remorse bit at him. But Father Eusebios, still flashing that same smile, looked at him and said, "Despite that long sermon you just delivered I still intend to visit Athens someday . . . God willing."

Stavro laughed.

The abbot touched him on the head with his fingers and said, "This is the first time I heard you laugh . . . perhaps the monastery agrees with you after all."

They started down.

Petro was waiting for them at the quadrangle gate. He was fuming. "Where have you been?" he yelled at both of them.

"We took a walk into the hills," said the abbot.

"You were gone almost an hour."

"I know. I am afraid it is my fault — your nephew and I had a long talk."

As they passed the chapel they heard the monks inside, praying. Their low voices seemed to be smothered by the dense silence that hung over the monastery. A pair of fragile blackbirds zoomed out of the sky and lighted on the branch of a lemon tree that stood before the door of Father Eusebios' cell.

"What did you talk about?" Petro asked them.

"God," said the abbot.

"Kyrie eleison! Who won?"

"It was not a battle." Father Eusebios looked at Stavro and smiled. Just then the bell clanged; slowly, the monks came squinting out of the church and walked in single file toward their cells. For a moment Stavro wondered what mysterious force kept these men here — day after day, their cramped lives wedged between mumbled prayers, fitful sleep, and a bite of stale bread.

"It is time to take this off," said Petro, wrestling out of his cassock. He handed it to Father Eusebios. Stavro took his off also. Suddenly Petro flung up his arms and cried, "I feel like a defrocked priest!"

The abbot laughed. "Come," he said, "I shall accompany you as far as Zachlorou."

"No," said Stavro. "There is no need . . . we know the road."

"But I want to . . . I insist."

"Give us your blessing, Your Grace," Petro said. "We ask for nothing more."

Father Eusebios brought up his thin hand and touched each of them on the head. "Go to the Good," he said. "God protect you . . . may He lead you to your priest . . ." Petro kissed his hand. The abbot tousled his hair and said, "Our door shall always be open to you."

"I may surprise you," Petro replied, grinning.

Turning to Stavro, the abbot said, "I offer you my hand, not as a priest, but as a friend. . . ."

Stavro seized it and shook it. Father Eusebios pulled him into his arms and embraced him. "I shall pray for you always," he said. "Perhaps we will meet someday in Athens . . ." he gave Stavro a wan smile.

All three walked silently across the quadrangle. Father Eusebios stopped at the gate to bless them once more, then, turning sharply around and without another word, he hurried back toward his cell.

4

"German trucks!" Petro cried out. "Look, four of them. . . ."

"Quick, behind these rocks," yelled Stavro. He pointed to a sharp ridge just off the road to the left. They ran to it and hid between two gaping boulders. Petro was breathing hard.

"There is no need to fear," Stavro said. "They did not see us."

Petro crawled in deeper and did not answer him. As the trucks thundered past them Stavro felt his body tighten — he peered over his shoulder and saw German soldiers jammed together, sitting stiffly on both sides of the trucks, their rifles wedged between their knees . . . white faces, sullen, cold.

"They are going toward the monastery!" Petro hissed into his ear.

"No, they will turn off."

But Petro crossed himself and cried, "God protect those ill-fated goatbeards . . . God protect them!"

Cautiously, Stavro crept out of the rocks and climbed to the highest point of the ridge. He could see the four trucks streaking in a direct line toward the monastery.

"There, you see," Petro was suddenly beside him. "They *are* going to the monastery!"

"Yes," said Stavro grimly.

"In the name of the Father . . . in the name of the Father!"

"Come, we must go back there," Stavro said.

Petro froze. "Have you lost your senses?" he exclaimed. "What can we do against that army?"

"Are you coming?"

"Kyrie eleison . . . of course I am coming!"

They kept away from the road and took a deserted goat path over a rock-infested hill. Lumps of dread began forming in Stavro's stomach — he tried to tell himself there was no reason for the Germans to harm Father Eusebios and his monks, but at the height of his hopes he heard the sharp sting of machine guns.

"Move!" he yelled to Petro.

His uncle had stopped and was leaning breathlessly against the trunk of a pepper tree. Again Stavro yelled at him, "I cannot wait for you . . . I am going alone!"

"No," said Petro, struggling to his feet. They were together when they reached the shadows of the monastery. Stavro was about to continue on, up the sharp road leading to the quadrangle gate, but Petro grabbed him by the arm. "Have you gone mad?" he cried.

"We can do no good sitting here on our hands," Stavro told him. But Petro would not let him go. He forced him into a narrow crevice and held him there until Stavro said, "Let me go."

"You will wait here until the Germans leave?"

"Yes," said Stavro.

Petro released him. Stavro lit a cigarette but tossed it away after a few puffs. Twice he thought he heard the trucks leaving but was wrong each time. He lit another cigarette.

"What is troubling you, Prometheus?"

"I do not like sitting here, waiting. . . ."

"I will tell you a story . . . a funny story."

"No!" Stavro barked at him.

Petro picked up a small twig and poked it into the ground. He acted as though he did not hear Stavro. " . . . We had a goatherd in Platano," he said, "whose name was Paminonda — the sun rose and set on his goats. . . ."

"I said not now!" Stavro yelled. But Petro plowed on. " . . . At that time, we young men of the village had our minds on skirts, if you follow me . . . but not Paminonda. He was too busy chasing his goats over the hills. Naturally, he was a bit

112

slow-witted and no one ever expected him to find a wife. But find one he did and as soon as he returned from his honeymoon, I cornered him in the coffeehouse and said to him, *'Paminonda, tell us all about your honeymoon.'* *'Yes, Paminonda,'* someone else chimed in, *'tell us what happened on your wedding night!'* Soon, everyone in the coffeehouse was on Paminonda's back. He scratched his hard head for a moment, then began, *'On Tuesday morning . . .'* *'No, no!'* we all cried out, *'begin from the first night, Paminonda — what happened Sunday night?'* Again Paminonda scratched his head and said, *'. . . On Tuesday morning . . .'* *'Aman, Paminonda!'* I yelled. *'Can you not force that mountain-goat brain of yours to function, just once? We do not care to hear what happened on Tuesday morning. Begin from Sunday night!'* But for the final time Paminonda scratched his head. With a trace of anger in his husky voice, he shouted at us, *'On Tuesday morning, my Marigo tapped me on the shoulder and said, "In the name of the Father, Paminonda — get off . . . we have not eaten in two days!"'"*

There was a long silence during which Petro kept jabbing the small twig into the ground. Suddenly they heard sounds; the four trucks came screeching down the road from the monastery. Petro leaped to his feet and cried, "They are leaving!"

Stavro waited until the trucks disappeared from view and then he started running wildly up the road. When they reached the gate a heavy pall of fear fell on him. Nothing moved in the quadrangle; not one monk was in sight! Every door along the cell row was flung open.

"In the name of God," shouted Petro, crossing himself. "Where is everyone?"

"The church," said Stavro.

They ran up the steps into the chapel; it was empty. Again Petro crossed himself and cried, "Something evil has happened . . . I can feel it!"

They tried the refectory. Nothing. Stavro could hear his heart beating viciously against his ribs. He could not think — there

113

was no other place to look . . . the church, the refectory, the cells . . .

They came out into the quadrangle again, not knowing which way to turn. The sky had grown very dark now; it started to rain. They ran into one of the cells. Stavro stood by the open door while Petro sat on the bed, mumbling out loud, "This is the Evil Hour . . . this rain, this dreadful silence . . . !"

"Did you look closely at the trucks?" Stavro asked him.

"Yes," said Petro.

"I mean, inside the trucks . . ."

"Yes, I saw only Germans."

"But the shots . . . we heard machine guns."

Petro stood up and came to the door. "Only God knows what happened here," he sighed, exhausted. He bent over the brazier and went to light it but Stavro stopped him. "We must go out and look for them," he said.

"In this downpour?"

"Yes."

"But we looked everywhere . . . !"

"I am going into the cliffs," said Stavro. He stepped outside. For a moment Petro hesitated at the door, then quickly followed after him, across the rain-splattered quadrangle, and through the gate. Every step was treacherous — the rain, the darkness, the cliffs — but they managed to reach the summit of the first hill. From here, Stavro had hoped to scan the narrow crevices below, but the rain was coming down so fast he could not see more than ten meters in front of him. He pointed to another hill and they started out for it. Petro cursed out loud every step of the way.

They climbed a sharp cliff whose sheer wall, blazoned with weird diagonals of razor-edged ribs, jutted out like the fins of a great fish. Except for the wind the sky was quiet. In the distance, lodged perhaps in some narrow crack of wall, two crickets started drilling at each other in shrill but steady notes. It was the same cliff Stavro had climbed that morning with Father

114

Eusebios. Although they had only a short way to go to reach the top, Petro suddenly refused to move.

"I will wait here for you, Prometheus," he grunted.

Stavro nodded.

"Do not take long . . . this place terrifies me."

Stavro found a break in the wall and got a good hold with his fingers. He pulled himself up and was relieved to find a wide gap between the wall, together with a long chain of rock shelves that brought him clear to the top of the cliff. Carefully, he crawled to the edge. At first, his eyes could not penetrate the rain and darkness but he did not move from there until he at last was able to make out the faint outlines of boulders and rocks far below him.

He heard a voice — a piercing, agonizing cry that seemed to come from the bowels of the earth. Thinking it was the wind, he waited. He heard it again — much louder and clearer. It was a man's voice, pain-wracked and hoarse. He ran back to Petro out of breath. "They are at the bottom of the cliff!" he shouted.

"Who?"

"The monks . . ."

"Are you sure?"

"Yes, I heard someone cry out. . . ."

"You did not see them?"

"It was too dark . . . come," said Stavro. They crept down the rock shelves together. When they got to the bottom they swung around the side of the cliff just as the same cry filled Stavro's ears again. He tried to follow its frightful wake but at this point the sky unburdened itself completely, soaking them to the skin.

"This is madness!" Petro grumbled. "Stavro, let us go back — we can do nothing for them now. . . ."

"No."

"Kyrie eleison, your head is like a block of marble. I tell you it is too late . . . they are all dead!"

Stavro went on alone. He did not get very far . . . deep in a hollow crater of rocks he found the first monk — a feeble old man, his head split, blood on his face, his beard, his robe . . . A few more meters and Stavro found another — he could not identify him . . . the face was drilled with bullet holes. A third. A fourth. . . He heard something behind him. Petro was on his knees, moaning beside the old monk.

"Get up," said Stavro.

"I was talking to him this morning," Petro wailed. "His name is Brother Chrysostomas . . . he talked to me about his village, his family, his first trip to Kalamata . . . he had the funniest laugh — like a goat. . . ."

Stavro went to lift him up but Petro slapped his hand away. He wiped his eyes. "Those bastards," he choked. "Those white-blooded bastards!"

Again, Stavro offered him his hand.

"Leave me alone!" Petro barked.

Stavro pushed on . . . Two more monks . . . young, lifeless, there at his feet . . . and just at their fingertips, his mouth wide open as though he were about to call out Stavro's name, lay Father Eusebios. His twisted, mangled body brought tears into Stavro's eyes. He knelt down and took the abbot in his arms, aware that his uncle was standing behind him.

"Is he dead?" said Petro.

"Yes."

Petro crossed himself. "I warned you not to come here."

Suddenly a young monk moved his head. He opened his mouth painfully. "Help me . . . !" he moaned. Stavro went to him. He cautioned him not to speak or move but the boy would not listen to him . . . he poured out everything . . . how Father Eusebios, cloaked in courage, came forward to meet the German trucks when they entered the monastery . . . how he offered them food and wine and asked them inside to rest . . . At first, the Germans appeared peaceful and in a joyous mood . . . but exactly at three o'clock the German officer in command ordered the soldiers to march the monks out of their cells, forcing all of

116

them to climb the cliff — even three old monks who were so ill they had to be carried . . . The young monk began sobbing hysterically when he told them how the Germans sent a cross-fire from their machine guns, ripping their bodies as they knelt there, praying.

He wanted to say more but blood started gushing from his mouth. He retched. Petro got up and walked away. The boy's face grew deathly white; he lifted his hand weakly and beckoned Stavro to take it. Before they could touch, he slumped into quiet death. Stavro leaned over and closed his eyes. For a moment he allowed his hand to rest on the boy's forehead — it was still warm. *In God's name, he felt he should say something . . . let the heavens know that here lies a dead youth in black robes and gold cross . . .*

"Stavro, please — let us get out of here!" Petro begged him.

"He is dead," said Stavro.

"I know, I know. . . ."

"What kind of a God is he . . . I cannot understand Him!"

"Come, Stavro."

" . . . He kills those who love him . . . What kind of a God is He?"

Petro grabbed him by the arm and pulled him up. But in a wild rage, Stavro pushed him away, "I am staying here," he cried.

"Stavro . . . no!"

"We must bury these men . . . we cannot leave them this way."

"Stavro, come to your senses — how can we possibly bury them in these rocks?"

"Go to Zachlorou. Get help."

"Come with me, Stavro."

"No, I will wait here for you."

"And who will help us from Zachlorou?"

"Go," said Stavro. "They will come when they learn what has happened here . . . go!"

117

Petro grunted. He did not take three paces before Stavro called out to him, " . . . And bring back a priest!"

5

After the burials, everyone gathered inside the refectory where the women of Zachlorou had prepared a sparing meal of chickpea soup and dark bread. Before eating, Pappa Yiorgo, the aged priest from nearby Rogous, blessed the food and also the large dish of sitari, the wheat of mourning. After the blessing Petro leaned forward and said to the priest, "Where I come from, Pappa, we have noble customs regarding death. Above all, we do not fear Charon. Perhaps you did not know this, but in the beginning Charon was on our side — he loved us very much. But let me tell you what happened . . . one day, God the Father sent Charon to earth to reap the soul of a young girl, but when he saw her stunning beauty and after he heard the pitiful lamentations of her family, he was overwhelmed with sadness and returned to Heaven without fulfilling his mission. God the Father asked him why he did not bring back the soul of the young girl and Charon replied he could not bear the agony that filled his ears and flooded his eyes. God the Father got angry and struck Charon many blows, rendering him deaf, blind, and lame. Thus, whenever he was sent to earth again on other missions he could not see whether the soul he was about to take belonged to an old man or a child . . . He was so deaf he could not hear the wailing and crying . . . and he could not run away because he was lame."

"That is a good story," Pappa Yiorgo said, nodding his head.

"It is not a story, Pappa — but the truth."

Pappa Yiorgo turned to Stavro and said, "I understand you are on your way to Kalavryta?"

"Yes," said Stavro.

"Perhaps you will pass by a small stream between Kleitoria

118

and Kalavryta . . . in truth, this is the River Styx, across which Charon transported his dead souls."

"We will be on the watch for it, Pappa," Petro exclaimed. "However, I am not prepared as yet to look Charon in the eye."

"That is true — you are still a young man."

"You flatter me, Pappa . . . I have had many meals from the table of life, if you follow me."

Clearing his throat, Pappa Yiorgo asked, "Did you know Father Eusebios well?"

"We were his guests for several days," Petro replied.

"You and your nephew?"

"Yes."

"What is your nephew's name?"

"Ask him . . . he is old enough to speak for himself."

"What do they call you, my son?"

"Stavro."

Pappa Yiorgo sighed. "It is a saintly name . . . it stands for the cross of Christ."

"And my name," cried Petro, "what does that stand for?"

"The rock. The solid foundation of our church . . . the one true confession of faith," the priest replied.

Petro scratched his head, "All that? And how about your name, Pappa?"

"Yiorgo was a man who labored in the earth . . . a tiller of the soil."

"I think God has bungled things up, Pappa. You, who should have a more Christian name, He calls *farmer* — and we, who are simple people, He calls *saints!* But getting back to what I started to say about death — I must admit, Pappa, I was not very pleased with the way you handled the situation here today."

The priest did not like this. "What do you mean?" he said.

"Priests and monks should not be buried as you buried those ill-fated men. It was not proper . . . not proper at all."

"What did I do that was wrong?"

"You treated them like laymen . . . by washing their bodies

in wine. Where I come from, Pappa, a man of God is not washed in wine but oil!"

"And just where do you come from?" Pappa Yiorgo exclaimed.

"Platano."

"Where is that?"

"The southernmost tip of Greece," said Petro with pride.

The old priest bit his cheek as though to keep from laughing. "You people indeed have strange customs," he said. "If I recall correctly, you did not accept Christianity until the ninth century."

"You are right, Pappa — we chew things very carefully before swallowing."

Again turning to Stavro, the priest said, "You are not saying much."

Stavro wanted desperately to light a cigarette but this was not the place. He grinned at the priest and said, "How far is Rogous from here?"

"For you, a short journey. But for me, two hours."

Stavro asked him if he knew anything about Pappa Lambro, but he said no. "I keep to my little village," he added. "I have not been to Kalavryta for many years."

There was a sudden commotion outside the door of the refectory. A young boy came running inside toward them — he was a spindly lad of about twelve. His large brown eyes danced with anxiety as he stood before Stavro. "There are two men outside," he cried. "They want to speak to you."

Petro's face paled.

"Who are they?" Stavro asked the boy.

"They did not say."

"What do they look like?"

"One is old, like my father . . . the other is very young. . . ."

"Like me?" said Stavro.

"No, younger."

Stavro pushed back his chair and got up. "Come," he said to

120

Petro. But Petro shrunk back in his chair, terrified.

"Come," said Stavro again.

"Stavro — I am afraid. . . ."

"There is nothing to fear — they are not Germans."

"No, you go."

"Perhaps they have a message for us," said Stavro. He took hold of his uncle's arm and led him outside. Petro refused to go farther than the steps. Suddenly a familiar voice filled the air: "Stavro . . . Stavro!"

They saw Kleanthi racing toward them from the gate, waving his hands frantically. Behind him came Kapetan Thanasi. Petro did not move from the steps as Stavro rushed to meet them. He swept Kleanthi into his arms and embraced him. "Kleanthi," he cried, "it is really you!"

Kleanthi was overjoyed and could not speak. Kapetan Thanasi offered Stavro his hand — his eyes were filled with tears. "How did you find us?" Stavro asked him.

"It was not easy," exclaimed Kleanthi.

"We will talk about that later," Kapetan Thanasi replied. He looked toward Petro, who was still on the steps, white-faced. Kapetan Thanasi waved to him; he called him down.

"What is it, Petro," he shouted out, "are you not happy to see us?"

"I have dreaded this day, friend Kapetan . . ." said Petro in a shaking voice.

"Petro, listen to me. . . ."

"No, you must first listen to me . . . I have something to tell you."

"I know," said Kapetan Thanasi.

"Yes," burst in Kleanthi. "They told us everything in Platano . . . !"

"They told you what I did to Panago?"

"Yes," said Kapetan Thanasi.

"Barba Spero was innocent, friend Kapetan. Panago was going to kill him and he was innocent!"

"I know," said Kapetan Thanasi. "I had a long talk with the elders of your village. You were right, Petro — every coin has two sides."

"Then you are not angry at me?"

"No."

"But I killed Panago . . . I shot him!"

Sensing that his uncle was on the verge of tears, Stavro interrupted them. "You did not answer my question, Kapetan," he said.

"What question?"

"How did you know where to look for us?"

"Forget it — the important thing is that we did find you."

"When you did not return from Platano," said Kleanthi, "we knew you were going to Kalavryta, Stavro — you talked about it so much."

"Any word about your priest?" said Kapetan Thanasi.

"Nothing."

"You have not gone into Kalavryta yet?"

"No," said Stavro.

"But we are well to the north of the city."

"We had to circle around it. There was trouble in Kerpini. . . ."

"Trouble?"

"The Germans lost an entire company . . . also seventy-two prisoners."

Kapetan Thanasi grunted. "Kapetan Costa works these hills . . . he is a lion of a man."

Petro asked him, "Friend Kapetan, did you happen to pass through Zachlorou?"

Kapetan Thanasi nodded his head grimly.

"Then you saw it with your own eyes . . . and now this! Is it worth it, friend Kapetan — really worth it?"

Kapetan Thanasi avoided answering him. He looked at Stavro and said, "We have come to join you."

"Join us?"

122

"Yes, into Kalavryta. . . ."

Stavro was vehement about it. "No — Pappa Lambro is our responsibility!"

"We are your friends — we are all in this together," said Kapetan Thanasi, visibly hurt.

Petro spoke out. "I say let them come — we need their help."

"No," yelled Stavro.

"It cannot be more dangerous for four than it is for two," Kleanthi said.

"The boy is right," said Kapetan Thanasi.

Stavro turned to leave but Kapetan Thanasi called him back: "Stavro, I have something to say to you."

"Speak."

"I must say it privately."

Petro took Kleanthi and walked into the refectory. Kapetan Thanasi tapped Stavro on the shoulder. "Come, walk with me around the quadrangle," he said. But Stavro could not wait.

"What is it?" he cried. "Has anything happened to my mother?"

Kapetan Thanasi's eyes flirted with him for a moment. "I had a long talk with Pappa Lambro's niece," he said, measuring Stavro sternly. Immediately, hot flames ignited inside Stavro's veins; his blood began to race. ". . . She is a beautiful girl — I envy you, Stavro. When she learned Kleanthi and I were in the village, she came to meet us. . . ."

Stavro was too flustered to speak.

"She is going to have a child, Stavro. . . ."

"She told you this?"

"Yes . . . she got very upset when she learned that you had gone to Kalavryta. I promised her I would keep my eye on you — that is why I am here."

Stavro grew silent.

"She does not appear to be troubled," said Kapetan Thanasi.

"By what?"

" . . . your not being married."

123

Stavro could not find the words to defend himself. He did not have to justify his life to anyone — even Kapetan Thanasi. Any other time perhaps he would have struck back, but now he wanted only Anna . . . to feel her in his arms, hear the new life inside her, beating against his heart. . . .

"I saw your mother also . . . she knows about the girl."

"You told her?" said Stavro.

"No, the girl did. . . ."

Stavro became very uneasy. He looked back, hoping to see his uncle and Kleanthi come walking out of the refectory. Long black shadows had quickly spread over the quadrangle. The air turned cold. At last, the door of the refectory opened. Kleanthi and his uncle were the first to come out. Kleanthi ran to Stavro and said, "Stavro, we met Anna . . . !"

Stavro roughed up his hair. "Yes, I know."

Kleanthi dropped his eyes. "I can see why you love her . . . she is a goddess."

Stavro put his arm around the boy's thin waist and together they walked across the quadrangle to the gate.

FIVE

PAPPA YIORGO accompanied them to Rogous.

The old priest rode sidesaddle on his gray donkey, a slow-moving yet never obstinate beast who seemed to know every inch of the way. Petro walked alongside the donkey and quickly engaged himself in a steady conversation with the priest. They were forced to move slowly since the place was choking with rocks and boulders. But the donkey plodded on and soon they were on a sloping goat path leading downward into a wide valley. They saw houses.

"Ah," cried out Pappa Yiorgo, "there is my little village!"

Petro laughed. "There is not much to it, Pappa."

The priest jabbed his finger into Petro's side and giggled. "The ancients always said: *'Greatness is never found in large numbers. . . .'*"

"You are right, Pappa." Petro patted the donkey on the neck. "You did not tell us your donkey's name," he said.

"Liaka."

"I had an uncle with that name . . . his father had a devil of a time with him. Liaka refused to work, but far worse than that, he had no desire for a woman. All day long he was stuck in the coffeehouse. *'Aman, Liaka,'* his father used to say to him, *'you are forty-four years old. You cannot go through life on cards and cigarettes . . . !'* But it was like speaking to a rock. One day they found Liaka stiff on the coffeehouse floor. His soul had burst out of him . . . he was dead. I swear he had so much cigarette smoke in his lungs, he could breathe only through the pores of his skin. But I ask you, how long can a man keep that up? Did not Christ once say: *'It is far better for a man to marry than to burn'?"*

Pappa Yiorgo corrected him: "It was Paul, not Christ."

"What is the difference," said Petro. "It is in the Bible, is it not?"

"Of course."

Pointing to Stavro, Petro yelled out, "You there, Prometheus — open your ears and listen . . . the same thing is going to befall you . . . Look at him, Pappa — I beg you . . . look at him . . . my voice is hanging in the wind . . . *he is lighting another cigarette!"*

"Do not scold the boy," said the priest.

"He is no boy . . . he is twenty-three years old!"

"You are too harsh on him. . . ."

Petro spat into the air disgustedly and dropped back to talk with Kapetan Thanasi. Stavro took hold of the donkey's rope and continued down the slope. Pappa Yiorgo tapped him gently on the head. "You rarely have much to say, my son."

Stavro kept walking, head down.

"Is something bothering you?"

"Nothing," said Stavro.

"Your face seems clouded with many thoughts."

"I was thinking about Father Eusebios. . . ."

"Ah, a wonderful man . . . a dedicated servant. It is a pity God called him so early in life."

"German bullets called him!" cried Stavro. Before he could prevent it the words had slipped out. The priest looked at him sternly. "Of course, my son," he murmured. "Of course."

They entered the village.

Three small boys came running toward them, waving their thin arms and shouting. Pappa Yiorgo gave them a hasty blessing and at the same time cautioned them to stand clear of the donkey. They did not listen to him. One of the boys grabbed hold of the donkey's tail and strutted behind it. The priest tried to shoo him off but the boy hung on. Stavro touched him on the head. "Heed your priest, little goat," he said. "He does not want you to get hurt."

Instantly the boy released his hold on the donkey's tail. He was not more than ten years old but he had the look of an old man . . . pale and wan, emaciated. He fell back with the other boys. All three circled around the donkey, shouting at it, teasing it . . . yet always managing to escape the frantic thrusts of the old priest's hands.

"If you do not stop," he warned them, "I shall report this to your fathers!"

They ran off without another sound.

"The little devils," cried Pappa Yiorgo, wiping his face with his handkerchief. "They do this everytime . . . you would think I was returning from Athens." He leaned forward and said to Stavro, "Did they hurt Liaka?"

"No," said Stavro. "They meant no harm."

Pappa Yiorgo measured him. "You have a manner with children," he said.

"What do you mean?"

"I saw the way you touched that boy on the head . . . how you spoke to him."

They came to a house. An old man opened the front door and hobbled out toward them — he waved his hand. He was toothless and white-haired. His thin dark face was grooved with many lines. Pappa Yiorgo gave him his blessing but did not stop. He prodded the donkey on, digging his heels into its sunken side. As they reached the heart of the village, more people came out of their houses to greet them. Two dogs picked up the scent of the donkey and rushed at it, barking. From behind his back Stavro heard his uncle say, "In the name of the Father, my head is spinning with all this noise. Pappa, where is your house? Take us to it quickly!"

The priest brought the donkey to a halt in front of a small white stucco house adjacent to the church. Immediately a crowd formed around them but Pappa Yiorgo begged them to step aside and let them pass through. Once inside his house, the priest slammed the door shut and cried, "Praise God . . . we are here!"

His wife was waiting for him near the door, wringing her hands around a soiled white cloth. She had a pot boiling on the jaki. She was a fragile gray-haired woman. As she stepped forward to greet her husband he drew back. He lifted his fingers and blessed her. "With God's help," he said, "I have returned."

"Did all go well at the monastery?" she asked him.

Pappa Yiorgo let out a deep sigh. "Not a soul was left alive . . . the beasts devoured them all!"

"The abbot also?"

"Yes."

"In the name of the Virgin . . . !" she cried, crossing herself.

"We are hungry," said Pappa Yiorgo, frowning.

She nodded her head and went to the jaki. Pappa Yiorgo slipped off his shoes and slumped into a chair next to the kitchen table. He motioned the others to sit also. Kleanthi however walked to the window to look at the crowd that was still milling about in the priest's yard.

Kapetan Thanasi teased him: "I know you are panting to go out there, Kleanthi." He grinned. "I saw those two young girls eyeing you. Very well, go . . . but mind you, do not stray!"

Kleanthi walked to the door. His strides were slow, deliberate, as if to show them he was not really anxious. After he was gone, Petro said to the priest, "You see, Pappa — nothing in the world can stand in the path of young love. You raise a son, bring him up properly, tell him to do this, do that . . . and for a while he listens to you. But when he feels that first throb of manhood under his flesh all your preachings fly out the window."

The priest took in every word. He made a sour face and replied, "You forget one thing . . . one very important thing."

"What is that?"

"This throb of manhood as you call it *can* be chained and brought under control."

Petro laughed. "By whom?"

"By God and His Holy Church . . ."

"We are not talking myths, Pappa — these are the facts of life. When a boy touches a girl for the first time God may as well sit on His hands."

The priest was getting nervous. He flitted his eyes toward his wife and cried, "When are we going to eat?"

"Soon," she replied. "Be patient . . ."

Petro kept after him. "Is it true," he said, "that the Bible tells us not to lust after a woman?"

"Yes, it is true."

"And does it not go even deeper than that?"

"What do you mean?" said Pappa Yiorgo.

"Did not Christ warn us we should not even think lustful thoughts?"

"He did, He did."

"Do you agree with Him?"

"Of course!"

"In other words, if I see a beautiful woman walking down the street, or in church, I am supposed to look the other way?"

"You are not to look at her with lust."

"But she is a beautiful woman — how else can I look at her?"

"Not with lust — otherwise it is a sin," the priest warned.

"We are getting away from the subject," said Petro. "We were speaking about an innocent boy and an innocent girl. Does Christ have to show His face here? No matter what we Greeks are involved in . . . whether it is eating, drinking, sleeping, making love, having children . . . dying, there is Christ knocking on

129

our door. Once, just once, can we not enjoy a little privacy?"

Realizing he was getting nowhere with Petro, the priest turned to Stavro. Almost apologetically, he said, "My son, we are simple people . . . we are born; we die. God never intended for us to wrestle with these problems. Men much wiser than ourselves have tried to find the answers but today they are dust, and God's law still prevails. . . ."

"What are you trying to say, Pappa?" Petro broke in.

"I was speaking to your nephew."

"Pappa, we are all in this together — my nephew does not sit on a higher throne because he studied philosophy in Athens."

Pappa Yiorgo's mouth dropped open. "I did not know this," he cried. His wife was trying to get his attention from the jaki, but Pappa Yiorgo tossed his eyes at her angrily and she went back to her work. Again turning to Stavro, he said, "I am overjoyed to hear this about you, my son. Philosophy is a wonderful subject — I have always maintained there is a close kinship between God's law and philosophy . . . do you not agree?"

"No," said Stavro. "They are entirely different."

"Why do you say this?" The priest looked at him, surprised.

"One seeks the truth," said Stavro, "the other claims it has found it."

"Are you implying that truth cannot be found?"

"First, it must be sought."

"Did not Moses seek it . . . Isaiah, Paul, Christ?"

"They declared it; they did not seek it."

Pappa Yiorgo flung his hands in the air. "We are playing with words," he shouted. He looked Stavro square in the eyes and said, "This is the danger that arises from books . . . *man's wisdom is foolishness in the eyes of God!* Unless you reconcile yourself to this, you will never be happy. . . ." Making it very plain he wanted no further part in the conversation, Pappa Yiorgo left the table and went upstairs. He did not return until his wife called him to eat.

They fell on the food like animals. No one spoke until the

130

plates were clean. It was Kapetan Thanasi who broke the silence. "Pappa," he said, "I am gravely concerned about your little village. I think you should warn your people to be on the alert."

"For what?" said the priest, cleaning his teeth with the nail of his little finger.

"The Germans work in a pattern . . . can you not see it? First, Zachlorou . . . then the Monastery of the Great Cave . . . it is obvious they have drawn a tight ring around Kalavryta and will not stop until every village in the area is destroyed. . . ."

The priest's wife crossed herself. "In the name of the Virgin," she cried, staring at her husband. But Pappa Yiorgo raised his hand and calmed her. "Why should they harm Rogous?" he said. "We have done nothing to irritate them. If they do come here, I have already instructed my people not to lift one finger. . . ."

"You make it sound quite easy," Kapetan Thanasi told him.

"Nevertheless, it is Christ's way," the priest replied. "We cannot destroy violence with more violence."

Petro boiled at this. "Kyrie eleison!" he yelled out. "We are not living in Jerusalem, Pappa . . . open your eyes — you saw what the Germans did to Zachlorou, also the monastery. What makes you think they will spare Rogous?"

"Christ will protect us," said the priest, unmoved. Again his wife crossed herself. Stavro got up and walked to the door.

"Where are you going?" his uncle asked him.

"For a walk."

"Do you want me to come with you?"

"No."

"I am afraid there is not much to see in Rogous," said Pappa Yiorgo. He got up from the table and opened the door for Stavro. "I shall start the vespers soon — if you wish, you can come to the church and light a candle."

Stavro walked outside. His uncle came with him as far as the porch. He put his hand on Stavro's shoulder and said, "Prometheus, you are in a strange village — keep your eyes peeled."

Stavro nodded his head. Petro did not say another word to him — he turned and walked back into the house. As Stavro hurried out of the priest's yard, he realized Kleanthi was no-where in sight. The boy had not joined them at supper and Stavro was concerned.

He would look for him.

It was a mild day for December. The sun had reached the highest part of the sky and was now descending rapidly. Toward the north, gray clouds were forming. Stavro did not see a soul on the narrow village street. It was better this way, he thought; for the past few weeks it seemed that life was spinning dizzily around in his head. Kapetan Thanasi's words still burned in his ears: *"She is going to have a child, Stavro. . . ."*

There were three women waiting outside the church for ves-pers to begin. They scowled a little when Stavro walked past them. One was a young girl, tall and fair-headed . . . perhaps not older than eighteen. She alone did not scowl at him. He kept walking, aware that she was watching him closely. The thought numbed him — he had not touched Anna in weeks and now; one young girl fills his eye and he is on fire. He walked faster, hoping to push her out of his mind.

He stopped in front of the coffeehouse. A few old men were inside, huddled around a table, playing cards. He stepped in. One of the men saw him and with piercing eyes asked him what he wanted.

"Is this not a coffeehouse?" Stavro said to him.

The man, obviously the proprietor, grunted. He was tall, very thin, and excessively nervous. He had the sleeves of his woolen shirt rolled up to his elbows, revealing the bulging blue veins in his arms.

"How do you want your coffee?" he asked Stavro.

"Medium . . . half-sweet," said Stavro. He pulled up a chair and sat down beside the card players. They did not speak to him. However, they screwed their faces tightly and kept squinting at him. The tall man brought the coffee — it was piping hot. Stavro sipped at it while the tall man stood over him.

"How does it suit you?" he asked Stavro, smirking.

"A little too sweet."

The tall man made a face. "I put hardly any sugar in it!"

Stavro took another sip. "You have a very friendly village," he said. He made no effort to pay the man.

"I will change it for you if you still think it is sweet," the tall man said, hovering over him.

"Forget it," said Stavro. He reached into his pocket and paid the man.

"What business do you have here in Rogous?" he asked Stavro.

"I am visiting a friend. . . ." Stavro took two long sips, then asked, "What are they playing?"

"Prefa." The tall man went back to his chair and rejoined the others. Gulping down the rest of his coffee, Stavro got up and walked to the window. He had a clear view of the church from where he stood — the fair-headed girl was looking intently in the direction of the coffeehouse. Stavro's heart pounded.

Just as he stepped outside, the church bell started clanging. The two women crossed themselves and slowly climbed the steps . . . for a moment the fair-headed girl lingered there, then, turning slowly, she too went inside the church. More women appeared on the street. They walked silently past Stavro, their heads down. Behind them came Pappa Yiorgo. When he saw Stavro, he called out, "Have you decided to join us after all?"

"Yes," said Stavro.

"Good," the priest replied, patting him fondly on the arm. They walked together into the church. Pappa Yiorgo continued on, into the altar. Stavro looked around him — he saw a place not too far from where the fair-headed girl stood. He hesitated, but only for a brief instant. With his blood racing he went and stood behind her.

133

Her name was Tina.

She came to him in the cemetery soon after vespers ended. He could not understand what had come over him, but he asked her in church, leaned over and whispered the words into her ear. She did not nod her head, or blush. She answered him by closing her eyes gently as though she did not want even the drowsy icons to know.

They found a warm place between two cypresses where the wind could not enter. The day was still mild although the sun had not far to go before losing itself behind the mountains. Stavro did not know how to begin. He asked her, "Was that your mother, standing beside you in church . . . ?"

Her voice was timid. "Yes."

"Does she know you are here?"

"Of course not," she giggled.

"Are you afraid?"

She shook her head, then cut off a small branch from the cypress and began writing on the ground with its sharp point . . . quick nervous scribblings that Stavro could not make out.

"What are you writing?" he asked her.

"Nothing." She glanced at him childishly.

"How old are you?" he said.

She jabbed the point of the branch harder into the earth and did not answer him. Stavro held his eyes on her — she had thick full lips, enormous brown eyes. Her hair was the color of wheat in harvest. Again he asked her how old she was.

"Sixteen," she said, then quickly added, "but I will be seventeen in the spring . . . on May the first. . . ."

"Your hair is very light."

She flushed. Nervously her hand went to her hair. She fingered through it several times before tossing it back with a sudden snap of her head. "My father and mother came from Macedonia," she said. "Everyone is blond there, and red-faced like Englishmen. . . ."

134

"I know," said Stavro.

"Where do you come from?"

"Platano."

"Where is that?"

"Many kilometers south of here . . . near Kalamata."

"What are you doing in Rogous?" She leaned forward and daringly brushed her hair against Stavro's cheek. He cupped her face in his hands and kissed her on the lips. She did not try to pull away. He did it once more, driven by the moistness of her mouth, the fresh smell of her skin. She squirmed in closer, allowing him to take her in his arms. The fullness of her breasts sent flames into his manhood. He kissed her hard on the mouth, the neck. She rubbed her body against his, all this time not saying one word. But when his lips at last found her breast she let out a deep sigh and wrapped her arms hungrily around his neck.

Suddenly Stavro drew back.

He brought his right hand up and slapped her on the cheek. The blow stunned her.

"Go back to your house!" he yelled.

She fell into tears and tried to grab hold of his arms, but he pushed her away. "Go!" he cried. He swept her back, almost knocking her to the ground. Mortified, she fumbled with her coat, but her fingers shook so badly she could not button it. More tears filled her eyes. Biting her forefinger vindictively she let out a piercing groan, turned, and disappeared through the cypresses.

When he was certain she was gone, Stavro slid to his knees and with his right fist clenched, began pounding the ground. He did not stop until the blood showed on his knuckles.

Later that night, as they sat in Pappa Yiorgo's kitchen eating, Petro cleared his throat loudly and said, "Pappa, while we are all here together, I want to say this: you are my witnesses . . . In the name of the Father, I vow to you that in three years time I shall return here. . . ."

"We will be honored to have you," said the priest.

"I am not looking for honors, Pappa — I have a sacred duty to perform and I want you to assist me."

"Speak . . . what is it?"

"I told you once before — it is not proper for men of God to be buried without first anointing them with oil. However, since the mistake has been made, we have no alternative but to wait three years. . . ."

"I do not follow you," Pappa Yiorgo said.

"The bones of Father Eusebios and his ill-fated monks must be dug up and anointed with oil . . . but before we do this, Pappa, one thing is very important. . . ."

"What is that?"

"We must inspect the bones carefully."

"Why?"

"To see if they turned yellow-brown . . . this tells us whether or not the abbot and his monks lived a good life."

"Is it necessary to know?"

"Of course."

"And if they lived a wicked life . . . ?"

"The bones do not lie, Pappa — I can see from the way you are looking at me that you doubt every word. Believe me, this is no joke . . . if Father Eusebios and his ill-fated monks lived a wicked life their bones will be black."

Pappa Yiorgo stroked his beard. It seemed he was trying hard to keep from laughing. "You people indeed have strange beliefs," he said. "But tell me, somehow I get the feeling you wish to do these things purely from curiosity."

Petro's face dropped. "Pappa, you hurt me," he said. "Such thoughts have never entered my mind. I want to return here out of the goodness of my heart; my faith in God compels me."

"Then do so," cried the priest, apparently satisfied. He patted Petro fondly on the head and added, "God willing, I shall see you in three years. . . ."

"It is a pity," said Petro, "we cannot seal this vow with a

drop of wine — however, water will have to do." He went to lift the glass but the priest stopped him, simultaneously giving a quick nod to his wife. She hesitated at first, but spurred on by Pappa Yiorgo's second nod, she went downstairs and came back holding a bottle in her hands. Petro's eyes danced. "Pappa," he cried, "you are a rascal!" He pinched the priest on the cheek, then grabbed the bottle; he pulled out the stopper and sniffed it. "Aman . . . it *is* wine. Now my vow can be properly sealed." He leaned over and filled the glasses. It was red wine. Arms outstretched, they all touched glasses and drank. Stavro finished his with one swallow. Petro saw this and said, "Hey, Prometheus — slowly!"

Stavro thirsted for more. He held out his glass as Petro reluctantly filled it again. "This is not water," he growled at Stavro. Stavro gulped this down also. Petro frowned. He gripped the bottle tightly and filled everyone's glass for the second time. It was a small bottle and after he was finished he held it upside down for Stavro's benefit — not one drop was left.

Stavro settled back in his chair and fingered his empty glass. His uncle started to say something to the priest, but Stavro did not listen — his mind plunged headlong into Platano . . . he tried to visualize what Anna might be doing at this moment — walking perhaps from the church to Pappa Lambro's house after vespers, or sitting in the kitchen eating supper with her aunt, or lying on her bed alone . . . doing all these things while his child lay nestled in her womb, sucking life from her lungs. He still could not believe it: first the eye, then the lips, finally the embrace . . . yet from this fleeting moment a new life was born, and no matter how hard Stavro tried to ignore it, God's hand was linked in his, making the miracle complete. . . .

His uncle was saying, ". . . Pappa, another thing that bothered me at the burials was the absence of the miroloy. . . ."

"The miroloy?"

"Yes. There can be no death without it."

"Did we not weep for the departed ones?" said Pappa Yiorgo.

137

"Weep did you say, Pappa? A dog weeps when he loses his master . . . goats weep when they are lost in the hills! Weeping is not enough. You cannot satisfy Charon with tears alone. He wants praise, Pappa . . . praise!"

Pappa Yiorgo began chewing his cheek. "I understand what you are trying to say, but I cannot agree with you. I journeyed to Tripoli one day when I was a student in the seminary. A relative had died and I went to assist in the burial service. I cannot describe my shock when one of the mourning women threw herself over the coffin and started in with that nonsense you call the miroloy."

"It is not nonsense, Pappa."

The priest glared at him, "It is far worse than nonsense — it is insanity!"

"I think Pappa Yiorgo is right," Kapetan Thanasi chimed in. "Although I am from Kalamata, where the miroloy has been practiced for many centuries, I must admit it has always repelled me. I see death as a natural conclusion to life — we should experience it in peace and quiet, without commotion."

"Death is no more natural than birth," Petro exclaimed. "We are thrown into it much against our wishes. It is a brave man who accepts this farce called life and death, who suffers along with it without complaining. Such a man deserves the highest praise . . . this is what the miroloy does for him."

"The dead can get along without such foolish hair-pulling," Kapetan Thanasi barked. "Besides, what good does it accomplish? Once God puts His finger to our name all the miroloys in the world cannot help."

"I do not agree with you, friend Kapetan," said Petro.

Here the priest murmured, "When a man dies we should beseech God to lighten his burden and lead him into eternal peace, far from pain and suffering. . . ."

"There is no pain and suffering in the hole!" Petro interjected sourly.

"I am speaking of the spirit," said the priest. "God's breath never dies."

In exasperation Petro cried out, "A Greek must make a big splash about everything. It is in his blood. I am surprised you do not understand this, Pappa. We had a man in our village who slaughtered a pig at the drop of a coin. He would lift the ill-fated squealing thing on his shoulders and carry it through the street, shouting: *I want everyone in the village to come to my house tonight . . . I am celebrating!'* Either it was his son's nameday or something else . . . his wife's pregnancy, his grandfather's birthday, his barrel of new wine . . . he loved to have people around him, to praise him and say good things about him. It is the same way with death — it is not proper for Charon to take us without a good word."

Pappa Yiorgo let out a loud yawn and got to his feet. "It is late," he said. "Tomorrow is Sunday and I must be at my best for the liturgy." He lifted his fingers and blessed them all. Looking at Stavro, he said, "We did not hear much from you tonight."

"All philosophers are given to moods, Pappa," Petro replied. But the priest, intent upon what he was going to say next, did not hear him. He touched Stavro on the shoulder. "Shall I see you in church tomorrow?" he asked him.

Before Stavro could answer, Kapetan Thanasi spoke out, "We shall all be in church tomorrow . . . after that, we go into Kala-vryta."

"So soon?" said the priest.

"Yes. We have work to do . . . work that cannot wait another day."

3

They were all seated at the kitchen table the next morning having coffee when Petro said, "Friend Kapetan, we are sitting ducks in this little village."

"I agree," said Kapetan Thanasi. "The sooner we lose our-selves in Kalavryta, the safer I shall feel."

The priest's wife went to the closet for more black bread and cheese. Stavro stopped eating to look at her — from the time they arrived in Rogous she had said very little. Humble, devoted to her husband, silent. The joy of simplicity seemed to fill her soul. Perhaps his mother was right after all, you can solve nothing by hurling questions at life. It is far better to lock horns with it and say: *"Thy will be done."* Yet, Stavro knew he could never do this — he was not blessed with meekness and humility as God had blessed this gentle woman who was leaning over him and placing more bread and cheese on his plate. He put his hand over hers and saw her flush.

"Pappa Yiorgo did not tell us," he said. "Do you have any children?"

She fumbled with a strand of gray hair that had fallen over her eyes. "No," she said. "I could not give him any."

Of course, Stavro thought, *blame yourself, little gentle woman — it is your own, your own grievous fault!*

Again Kleanthi was not eating. Petro teased him. He said, "Little goat, where did you run off to this afternoon?"

Kleanthi's face got red. "I met a few young boys," he said. "We talked, and then we went for a walk. . . ."

Petro slapped his thigh and roared, "The little goat has learned how to lie . . . did you hear that, friend Kapetan? They went for a walk . . . all boys!"

Before leaving the table Kapetan Thanasi said to them, "We are taking communion today."

"Again?" cried Kleanthi.

"What is this twisted passion you seem to have for com-munion, friend Kapetan?" said Petro.

Kapetan Thanasi gave him a stern look but Petro kept at it. "You cause me to wonder about you, friend Kapetan . . . did you have an unpleasant childhood . . . a tyrant for a father, a saint for a mother . . . ? These sort of things can easily make

140

a fanatic out of you. Or perhaps you are a frustrated goat-beard?"

Still glaring at him, Kapetan Thanasi snapped, "Life is measured from day to day, hour to hour. No one knows when the Bridegroom will come . . . I do not want Him to find us unprepared."

"You know your Bible well, friend Kapetan, but I think you are overstressing the point. Christ is not that severe. Surely, He makes allowances in time of war."

Kapetan Thanasi put on his jacket and walked to the door. He opened it, then glanced back. "We all shall take communion," he repeated. "I will meet you in front of the altar when the liturgy is finished." With this, he walked out. Stavro followed him. Petro and Kleanthi lingered for a while in the kitchen, then came out also.

Although the morning was sun-drenched, the air felt cold and sharp. As they walked down the street the church bell clanged. People poured out of their houses, crossed themselves, and headed quickly for the church.

Once inside, Stavro could feel many eyes on him. He looked everywhere but did not see the tall fair-headed girl. Mahogany benches lined the two sides and back wall of the church. However, most of the congregation chose to stand.

Pappa Yiorgo did all the chanting himself. He sped through the matins and was half-finished with the liturgy when the front door of the church suddenly burst open. German soldiers swarmed inside. With automatic rifles held high they worked their way through the congregation and into the altar. A half-dozen stood guard by the door.

Stavro felt his uncle's hand trembling on his shoulder. "In the name of the Father . . . !" Petro whined. "In the name of the Father."

There was a brief scuffle inside the altar. The Beautiful Door slid open and Pappa Yiorgo came out flanked by two young German soldiers. Stavro's hand went into his pocket. He ran his fingers over the cold surface of his revolver and followed the German captain closely as he climbed up the ambon steps. He was a short, squat man but he stood erect; he spoke in a deep guttural voice:

"Greeks of Rogous, we do not want to harm you. We desire only to talk to the men and boys. No one will be hurt. Women, take your daughters and return to your homes — immediately!"

A fearful wave of screams and groans rolled over the congregation. Again Petro gripped Stavro's arm.

"Stavro," he cried. "They are going to slaughter us!"

Kleanthi's face turned white. He kept looking at Kapetan Thanasi but the Kapetan was busy counting German heads. From the corner of his mouth he whispered to Stavro, "I make out twelve . . . do you have your revolver?"

"Yes."

"Good — I too have mine. Kleanthi is without . . . your uncle also."

"Perhaps they will not harm us," Kleanthi said in a quivering voice. Deep grooves formed over Kapetan Thanasi's forehead. "I do not know how we can do this," he said to Stavro.

"Look," cried Kleanthi. "They are forcing the women outside . . . !"

"Keep your voice down," Kapetan Thanasi cautioned him.

Only a few dozen men and older boys were left in the church. Again, Kapetan Thanasi counted heads. "I see only nine," he said.

"Three went outside with the women," Stavro replied.

The German captain remained on the ambon. He took out a cigarette and lit it, exhaling a thick cloud of smoke at the ceiling toward the icon of God's eye. Pappa Yiorgo, enraged, started to say something to him but one of the German soldiers at his side jabbed the butt end of his automatic into the priest's ribs and ordered him to stay quiet.

Finally, the captain stepped down from the ambon. He was met by another officer, a tall, sickly-thin lieutenant with

142

glazed eyes and slouched shoulders. They spoke into each other's ear. At last the captain turned and looked at the priest, "Tell these men not to fear," he said. "I want them to file out of the church three at a time . . . we shall be watching them — if they try to escape they will be killed!"

"What do you want with them?" Pappa Yiorgo cried.

"We wish to ask them a few questions," the captain replied, still puffing on his cigarette. "You have my word as a German officer — they shall not be harmed."

The captain stepped forward and pointed his finger at three men. Hands clasped together fearfully, Pappa Yiorgo pleaded with him again, but the captain gave him a tired look and ordered two soldiers to take the men outside. The priest came after them screaming, "These are innocent people . . . they have wives and children . . . !"

The captain calmly took out his revolver and fired. Pappa Yiorgo slumped to the floor, blood gushing from a gaping hole in the back of his head.

Like a raging beast Kapetan Thanasi leaped to his feet. One shot from his revolver brought down the captain. Three more shots and the soldiers guarding the three Greeks dropped to their knees, each clutching his stomach. One of them was in great pain. The sickly lieutenant took aim at Kapetan Thanasi with his revolver but before he could fire, Stavro pumped two quick shots into his head.

The Greeks fell to the floor of the church, fear-stricken. An old man crawled to his knees and tried to run for the door but three blasts from an automatic rifle blew half his head away. The same rifle turned and began hurling its fire into the wailing Greek faces huddled together on the floor. Stavro emptied the rest of his revolver; the rifle blasts stopped. In that instant Kapetan Thanasi raced across the floor, pulled away the rifle from the dead German's hands, and quickly fired at the two soldiers hiding behind the Holy Table in the altar, killing them both. There were two others hidden in the altar, but they were too terrified to shoot. They dropped their guns and came walking toward Kapetan Thanasi, hands high above their heads. With a fierce cry he turned upon them and emptied the rifle in their stomachs.

It was over.

Again, Kapetan Thanasi began counting German heads. "Nine," he said to Stavro.

"There are still three outside," Stavro told him.

"Where is your uncle?"

"I do not know."

One by one, the Greeks of Rogous got to their feet. Stavro searched each face but he could not find his uncle or Kleanthi. The wailing and groaning grew louder. Some of the men started for the door but Kapetan Thanasi ordered them back.

"My wife and two daughters!" one man cried out. He made a desperate lunge. Kapetan Thanasi grabbed him by both arms and held him. The man pleaded with the Kapetan. "I must go to them . . . !" he whimpered.

"In time," Kapetan Thanasi told him. When the man calmed down, Kapetan Thanasi let him go. Stavro meanwhile edged his way closer to the wounded men — three were already dead. Two others had severe bullet holes in their stomachs and were bleeding badly. The last, a young boy of about sixteen, was struck only in the leg. Petro and Kleanthi were nowhere in sight.

Kapetan Thanasi climbed a bench and looked out the window. After a while he motioned Stavro up also. "They have disappeared," he exclaimed, pointing toward the road.

"They will be back," said Stavro. He stepped down from the bench and was about to return to the wounded when he saw his uncle crawl from under the Holy Table. Behind Petro came Kleanthi. Stavro ran to them.

"Are you hurt?" he asked his uncle.

Petro's face was white; his hands shook. "Have they gone?" he said.

"Yes."

"Are you certain?"

"Nine Germans are dead . . . three ran off," Stavro said. He looked at Kleanthi. "Are you all right?"

"Yes." He too was white-faced. "Stavro," he said, "I did not have a gun . . . I had to hide. . . ."

"It is all right," Stavro told him. "Do not think about it."

Suddenly Petro saw the lifeless body of Pappa Yiorgo lying in a small pool of blood. "In the name of the Father!" he cried. His knees buckled. "Is God blind?" he groaned. "Why did He allow such a thing . . . why?"

Kapetan Thanasi came rushing toward them.

"Stavro," he said, "there is very little time. Summon everyone in the village — tell them to flee into the hills. Take your uncle and Kleanthi . . . go!"

Stavro did not move. "I am staying here," he said.

"There is nothing for you to do here."

"You go . . . I am staying."

"But why?"

"I must bury the priest."

"In God's name, Stavro — there is no time!"

"I cannot leave him this way . . . they will burn the church down when they come back." Stavro walked over to where Pappa Yiorgo lay — he bent down and lifted the priest in his arms. Kleanthi held the door open for him as he carried Pappa Yiorgo down the steps and across the churchyard, into the cemetery. He placed him carefully on the ground between two tall cypresses, realizing too late that it was the exact spot where he had kissed the fair-headed girl. He ran back to the church for a shovel.

Kapetan Thanasi and the others were gone. Both men who had been bleeding from the stomach were now dead. The young boy wounded in the leg had crawled away from the dead bodies and was sitting painfully against the leg of a bench. He was crying.

"Does your leg hurt?" Stavro asked him.

"A little."

Stavro bent over him. The bullet had passed through the shin bone just above the ankle — it did not appear to Stavro that the leg was fractured, although it was bleeding badly. He took out his handkerchief and tied it around the wound. Straightening up, he said, "I shall come back in a few minutes to make a splint for your leg."

Some of the fear left the boy's face.

"What is your name?" said Stavro.

"Mitso."

"I will not be long . . . do not move from here," Stavro told him. He passed through the altar, then downstairs into the cellar. He found a shovel hanging against the brick wall. An uneasy feeling crept over Stavro as he started back upstairs — it did not look like God's house: this place laden with rubbish, with broken benches, melted-down candles tossed everywhere . . . dirty-faced icons thrown to the ground, stamped upon, useless, never again to be kissed. . . . But it was the smell that bothered him most — stale death putrefying the beams above his head, saturating the walls, the ground . . . decaying death!

He had to hold his breath until he got back to the altar. Mitso had not moved. Stavro touched him on the head and said, "I am taking you with me — come, let me help you."

The boy tried to stand on his good left leg but he was too weak and toppled backwards, striking his head on the bench. It was not a hard blow and did not hurt him. Stavro handed him the shovel, then picked him up and carried him out of the church. He did not bring him into the cemetery; instead he eased him down beside the iron gate and said, "Stay here, and do not make a sound."

"What are you going to do with the shovel?" Mitso asked him. Stavro took the shovel from the boy and hurried through the gate without answering him. He worked frantically, aware that Pappa Yiorgo's frozen eyes haunted him. Like a sudden shift in the wind the priest's words came back to him:

146

"We cannot destroy violence with more violence . . . !"

He got the hole dug then stepped out to wipe the sweat from his face. Suddenly he was oppressed by guilt — was this a dead dog he was burying . . . a neglected dead dog? And what about the priest's wife . . . who would tell her?

Getting down on his knees to brace himself more firmly, Stavro rolled the priest into the hole. He covered it quickly, then marked it well by placing a large rock over it. He was weak from exhaustion when he returned to Mitso.

"You forgot the shovel," the boy said to him.

"Come," said Stavro in a tired voice. "Get up."

"When are you going to make a splint for my leg?"

"Later . . . after we get into the hills."

"Are you not going to bury the others also?"

"Give me your hand," said Stavro.

The boy started to cry. He turned his face away from Stavro and blurted, "That was my father. . . ."

"What are you trying to tell me?" said Stavro.

"He was the last to die . . . the one who was shot in the stomach. . . ."

"He was your father?"

"Yes."

"Why did you not tell me sooner?"

Mitso clamped his lips together, terror-stricken. He tried to get to his feet but Stavro eased him back down. "Stay here," he said.

"Where are you going?" said Mitso.

"To bury your father."

"No!"

"You do not want me to bury him?"

"My mother must see him first. . . ."

"It is too late . . . she cannot see him now." Again Stavro started to leave.

"I do not want you to touch him!" Mitso cried out. Tears began streaking down his face again. Stavro waited until he stopped crying and then said, "The Germans will not lose any time . . . they will be back any moment now. They will burn the church; they will set fire to every house in the village. Are you listening to me?"

"I am listening."

"Wait here," said Stavro. "I will not take long."

"No!"

"Do you want your father to burn?"

"My mother must see him first. . . ."

"They will burn him," Stavro yelled, getting angry now.

"I want my mother to see him . . . she must see him!"

Stavro heaved out a sigh. He reached down and took the boy's hand, but Mitso pushed it away and got up by himself. "I do not need your help," he said. He took one step, stumbled, and was about to fall — but Stavro grasped his arm and held him. "Here," he said, "put your arm around my shoulder . . . we shall walk together."

At first Mitso balked, but when Stavro refused to let him go he gave in and slowly put his arm over Stavro's shoulder.

"Keep off your bad foot," Stavro cautioned him.

The boy nodded. Together, they hobbled across the churchyard, into the street. Stavro stopped in front of the coffeehouse to look at Mitso's leg — the handkerchief was still firm and showed very little blood.

They moved on.

Mitso leaned more of his weight on Stavro and walked faster. When they were out of the village Stavro asked him where he lived.

"We have a farm in the hills," the boy replied. "My father . . . my father is a goatherd. . . ." He seemed uncertain when he said, *"is."* They came to the goat path and Mitso told Stavro they should follow it. "It will lead us to the chapel of the Prophet Elias," he said.

"How do you know we are going there?" Stavro asked him.

"I heard your Kapetan tell you in church."

148

He went on to say he knew every inch of ground in these hills, since he came here often with his father's goats. Stavro was pleased to hear the boy talk and nudged him on. He then told Stavro about his oldest brother, Nikko, explaining how he was the first Greek from Rogous to die in Albania . . .

He talked rapidly and did not want Stavro to interrupt him. When they reached the crest of a small ridge that was lined on both sides by immense boulders, the boy stopped and sat on a stone. His face had grown very pale. Stavro quickly bent over him and looked at his leg — the handkerchief was soaked in blood. He untied it and saw fresh blood gush out of the wound.

"Do you have a handkerchief?" he asked the boy.

"No."

Stavro unbuttoned his jacket, then his shirt. He tore off one corner of his undershirt and from that ripped off two pieces. One he put into his jacket pocket; he wrapped the boy's leg with the other. The bleeding did not stop, however. Stavro took the other piece of cloth and tied it around the upper part of the boy's leg, near the knee, twisting it around his hand several times. It was as though he had turned off a faucet — the bleeding stopped. Quickly, from a nearby scrub pine, he broke off a branch and inserted it between the knot on the cloth.

"Can you hold this?" he asked Mitso.

Mitso took the tourniquet and turned it tighter. "Yes," he said.

"Hold it as tight as you can bear," Stavro said. He helped the boy to his feet. They started up the goat path together.

"How long must I hold it?" Mitso asked.

"I do not know . . . I will release it every fifteen minutes or so," Stavro replied.

They straddled the ridge and worked their way down, into a sloping valley of white bedrock. Stavro kept looking at the boy's leg every few paces. He noticed that Mitso was putting more pressure on it and the bleeding had stopped completely.

"We should be there soon," said Stavro.

149

"Where?"

"The chapel of the Prophet Elias."

"I hope my mother will be there. . . ."

"If I know Kapetan Thanasi, he has summoned the whole village," said Stavro. "I am sure your mother will be waiting for us."

The boy's face brightened. He started walking faster.

"How much farther is it?" Stavro asked him.

"One or two cigarettes," Mitso replied.

They came face to face with another sheer wall of rock. Mitso led him around it and into a narrow, rock-cluttered gorge no wider than Stavro's shoulders. It got even more narrow when they sliced their way through it. Above them eaves of wet shiny rock sparkled with tiny stalactites that kept dripping down upon them in perfect sound and rhythm.

"I come here often in the summer to cool off," Mitso said. "The goats love it. There is a spring of cold water farther down . . . it is so cold it freezes your teeth. . . ."

Eventually the walls broadened. They saw the sky. A familiar voice found Stavro's ears: "Hey, Prometheus — you made it at last!"

He saw Petro standing beside Kapetan Thanasi; they were both waving at him and smiling. Kleanthi saw him and came running. Huddled around the small white chapel were several dozen people, most of them women and children. One of the women let out a loud scream when she saw Mitso. She fell upon him with tearful kisses. She embraced him, stroked his face and neck — kissed him on the cheeks again. Mitso tried to speak to her but she clamped her hand over his mouth fearfully. Stavro went to her and said, "His leg is not broken . . . wash it well and I will put a new bandage on it."

She looked at him with grateful eyes. Stavro patted Mitso on the head and left him with his mother. He walked to where Kapetan Thanasi and his uncle stood. Kleanthi had disappeared.

"Did you bury the priest?" Kapetan Thanasi asked him.

150

"Yes."

"Was there any trouble?"

"None."

"The Germans did not return?"

"No."

"Where did you find the boy?" said Petro.

"In the church . . . he was hit in the leg."

Petro scowled. "From the way his mother acts, you would think she had not seen him for years. . . ."

"The boy's father is dead," said Stavro.

"Which one was he?" asked Kapetan Thanasi. There was pain in his voice.

"One of the men who was hit in the stomach. . . ."

"I did not think he would make it," Petro said. "I have a theory about these things . . . a man's strength can also be his most vulnerable spot — I mean the stomach and the head. . . ."

"Shut up!" yelled Stavro.

"What is eating you, Prometheus?"

"I told you to shut up!"

Kapetan Thanasi stopped them. "Come," he said. "This is no time for words. We have work to do . . . much work." He led them into the crowd of sad faces. In the bright sunlight the little chapel gleamed; its gold cross was weatherbeaten and chipped around the edges. It suddenly seemed strange to Stavro not to have Pappa Yiorgo here.

Kapetan Thanasi saw Kleanthi and told him to post himself on a high rock behind the chapel. An old man piled together a few pieces of wood and started to light a match. Kapetan Thanasi angrily kicked everything away. "No fires!" he cried.

The old man shrugged and walked away.

"Hey, friend Kapetan," Petro called out. "How long must these ill-fated people hide in this Godforsaken place? Do you not feel an ounce of pity for them? They cannot stand the cold . . . they are old and feeble. Their children are weak. Where shall we find food for such an army?"

151

Kapetan Thanasi frowned. "We shall not be here very long."

"Why do you say that?"

"I know the Germans . . . they will waste no time."

"I hope you are right, friend Kapetan . . . for their ill-fated sakes, I hope you are right."

Stavro remembered Mitso and hurried back to him. He found him inside the chapel — the boy's mother had washed the wound and was holding a thick wad of cloth over it, pressing it down hard. Mitso was lying on the floor.

"Do you have more cloth?" Stavro asked her.

She handed him several pieces. He kept one and gave her back the rest. Bending down he took a closer look at the boy's leg — it was still bleeding. He was about to start with the bandage when he felt a hand on his left shoulder. Kapetan Thanasi held a flask in his hand and was offering it to him.

"Brandy," he said.

"Good," said Stavro. He unscrewed the top and poured a little over the wound. Mitso stiffened but did not cry out. Quickly, Stavro bandaged the leg. When he finished, he lifted the boy and carried him to a bench near the altar. He made him lie down.

"Cover him well," he told Mitso's mother.

"Shall I be able to walk?" Mitso asked him.

"Not for a few more days," said Stavro. Turning to the boy's mother again, he said, "He must stay off his feet for two or three days . . . it is very important."

She understood and nodded her head. Catching him off guard, she leaned over and kissed him on the cheek. Her eyes were wet with tears.

"I am sorry about your husband," Stavro said.

Again she nodded her head. She gave a frightened look at her son, then started weeping again. Stavro left them. Outside, the people of Rogous had formed into small groups: families with families, friends with friends. Stavro's heart went out to them. They did not speak nor weep. They stood there as though in a trance, eyes fixed at each other or upon the ground. From their midst Stavro saw his uncle coming toward him with anger in his eyes.

"Prometheus," he cried out, "I do not like it when you speak to me as you do . . . am I a donkey?"

Stavro turned his back on him.

"I am your uncle . . . your father's brother. Can you show no respect to me?"

Still Stavro would not answer him.

". . . What could I do in that church? I had no gun, nothing. Did you expect me to fight the Germans barehanded? Speak. Is this what you wanted me to do?"

"Leave me alone," Stavro yelled at him.

Petro let out a curse and sulked off, red-faced and growling to himself.

Stavro felt a sudden fatigue creeping over his body. He realized he had eaten nothing all day. He saw an old woman sitting on a small stone near the chapel, struggling frantically with a hard crust of black bread. She had no teeth and was trying to soften it first with her lips and tongue. When she saw Stavro she smiled and offered him a bite but he shook his head and walked away from her. He had a strong desire to go off somewhere — to sit and think of Anna . . . but in that instant he heard Kleanthi shouting from the ridge.

Stavro ran to him. From the bottom of the ridge he yelled up to him, "What is it, Kleanthi?"

The boy beckoned him to climb up. When he got there he followed Kleanthi's pointing finger: huge billows of black smoke were pouring into the sky. Every house in Rogous was in flames. Already the church had melted to half its size. Kapetan Thanasi joined them, panting; his eyes winced with pain as he said, "You see, they wasted no time . . . no time at all."

Soon all the villagers had climbed the ridge. Not one sound escaped from their lips as they watched their church and homes go up in smoke and flame. Stavro heard his uncle say to Kapetan Thanasi, "When the world comes to its fateful end, friend Kapetan, it shall not be as the goatbeards have taught us . . . weeping and gnashing of teeth, dead bodies rolling out of their graves, angels flying everywhere, and Christ sitting on His throne in the middle of it all, eager to judge each and every one of us . . . no, my friend Kapetan, it will not be that way at all! The world is going to burn itself into ashes. Every last one of us will be fried to a crisp . . . just like that poor ill-fated village!"

4

Early the next morning Kapetan Thanasi drew them aside and told them they must go into Kalavryta immediately. Petro alone objected. "If we go there," he warned, "we throw ourselves willingly at the Germans' feet."

"Kalavryta is a large city," Kapetan Thanasi replied.

"I do not like it, friend Kapetan."

"Have you forgotten why we came here?" Stavro snapped at him.

"He speaks . . . at last Prometheus speaks!"

"This is no time for joking," cried Kapetan Thanasi.

Petro was obstinate. "Friend Kapetan," he said, "listen to me — we can do Pappa Lambro no good if we get ourselves killed in Kalavryta. Not only that, but where are we to look for him . . . have you stopped to consider this?"

"If your priest has life we shall find him," said Kapetan Thanasi.

"Words, friend Kapetan . . . words!"

"No one is forcing you to come," said Stavro.

"Prometheus, you have eaten my liver these past few days. Have I said I do not want to come? I am just as anxious to find Pappa Lambro as you."

"Then why all the questions?" Kapetan Thanasi measured him sternly.

Petro shrugged. "I do not think we should go into Kalavryta this minute. I say wait a day or two — it takes a long time for the German to cool his head."

"It is decided," Kapetan Thanasi barked. "There is nothing further to discuss. We leave right away!"

Stavro started to walk toward the chapel.

"Where are you going?" Kapetan Thanasi asked him.

"To see the boy."

"It is best we leave without goodbyes."

Stavro hunched his shoulders. He reached into his pocket and pulled out the revolver. Snapping it open, he said to Kapetan Thanasi, "I have run out of cartridges."

"Look in my sack," Kapetan Thanasi answered. "I have ample boxes."

Stavro took out a box, loaded his revolver, then went to hand back the rest of the box.

"Keep it," Kapetan Thanasi told him.

Stavro shoved the box into his jacket pocket. All this time he could see that Kleanthi was itching to say something.

"What is it?" Stavro asked him.

Kleanthi pouted and said, "Why cannot I have a revolver also?"

"There are only two," said Stavro.

"Kapetan Thanasi has a third in his sack . . . I saw it."

Stavro turned to Kapetan Thanasi. "Is this true?" he asked.

"Yes."

"Then give it to him."

"No."

"Three guns are better than two, friend Kapetan," Petro exclaimed.

"I will gladly give it to you — but not the boy," Kapetan Thanasi replied.

"Kleanthi asked you first," said Petro, his voice shaking. Kapetan Thanasi stooped over his sack and dug out the revolver. He handed it to Petro, who refused to touch it. Grunting loudly, Kapetan Thanasi tossed it back into his sack. He buttoned it down then slung it over his shoulder. Kleanthi was downcast — he jabbed the toe of his boot into the ground. There was a small stone lodged there but he could not get it out. Without lifting his head, he said to Kapetan Thanasi, "I do not like to hide under church benches. . . ."

"Kleanthi, do not be impatient. . . ."

"Why did you ask me to come with you? . . . I am doing no good here."

"When we get back to our cave, I promise you, I will give you the revolver."

"The Kapetan is right, little goat," said Petro, tapping Kleanthi on the head with his finger. "We have a long road before us . . . cross yourself and ask God to guide us safely back."

But this did not satisfy Kleanthi. He was on the verge of tears. Stavro looked him straight in the eye and said, "Kleanthi, you must not feel this way. You are important to us — we need you very much."

"No, you do not need me!" the boy sobbed.

"But we do, Kleanthi . . ."

"Do not lie to me, Stavro. I have been no use to you . . . no use at all."

Kapetan Thanasi grunted. "Enough of this foolishness. Come, pick up your sacks, all of you. . . ."

"Are we leaving here, friend Kapetan . . . *pftt,* just like that?" said Petro, perplexed.

"I do not believe in goodbyes and tears," Kapetan Thanasi replied.

"You know best, friend Kapetan."

They moved out quickly.

It was still dark — morning had not broken as yet. Before they entered the narrow gorge Stavro tossed one final glance toward the chapel. Petro saw him and said, "I feel like a thief in the night — what will those ill-fated souls say when they awake and find us gone?"

156

"They will cry for a moment — but only for a moment," Kapetan Thanasi exclaimed. "Life goes on, friend Petro. No matter how hard we try to cling to it, life goes on!"

"Perhaps you are right, friend Kapetan, but I still do not like it. For the first time in my life I can understand how Judas felt."

It was pitch-black inside the gorge. They had to move slowly. When their eyes got accustomed to the darkness Kapetan Thanasi told them to join hands — this way they managed to proceed swiftly until at last they reached the other entrance to the gorge. Through the tight slit of rock above their heads Stavro saw a raw gray sky painfully awakening and rubbing the night from its unwashed face. Leading the way, Stavro passed around the sheer wall of rock, into the long sloping valley of white bedrock. Below them, in full view, lay Rogous — mired in its dry blood . . . the last breath of life stamped out of its lungs. Not one house was left standing; the church was a pile of ashes.

As they approached the smoldering ruins Petro crossed himself. He leaned over, picked up a handful of ashes and kissed them. Tears filled his eyes.

"Why did you do that?" Kleanthi asked him.

In a choking voice, Petro said, "These are human bones, little goat . . . It is not proper for them to die without a last kiss."

Kleanthi wrinkled up his face. "Why did you not take the revolver when Kapetan Thanasi offered it to you?"

Petro shook his head. "Little goat, someday you might understand. . . ."

"Understand what?"

"That you cannot snuff out a man's life as you would swat a fly on a wall. . . ." But Kleanthi was not listening to him. "I shall have that revolver," he said. "I shall have it before we return to the cave. I will reach into Kapetan Thanasi's sack when he is not looking, and I will take it . . . I do not care what he says!"

Petro would not take his eyes away from the pile of ashes. It did not seem to bother him, having Kleanthi watch as he cried.

157

Kapetan Thanasi moved well ahead of them. Every so often he kept looking back, trying to spur them on. Stavro grabbed hold of his uncle's hand. "The Kapetan is waiting for us," he said.

Petro said bitterly, "Of course . . . let us move forward, Prometheus! *Let the dead bury their own dead —* we have no business here. To Kalavryta! God only knows what lies in store for us there. . . ."

"What is wrong with you?"

"Everything is wrong. Can you not see it with your own eyes, Prometheus? The world is tilting again . . . that damn cursed scale! We cannot get away from it."

"Are you all right?"

"I am fine . . . fine!"

"I do not like to see you crying in front of Kleanthi."

"I am not ashamed."

"It is not a question of being ashamed. A young boy does not feel comfortable when he sees a grown man crying."

"Prometheus, my heart is heavy enough with grief without your foolish advice."

Before leaving him Stavro had one final word: "Uncle Petro, we are at Kalavryta's doorstep. Try to be strong. Another day or two and it will be over. Before you realize it we shall be on our way back to Platano."

"With Pappa Lambro?"

"Yes, God willing," said Stavro.

"What did you say?"

"I said, God willing . . ."

Petro snorted, "I have never heard you speak this way, Prometheus. Can it be you are admitting defeat?"

"Defeat?"

"Yes, to God."

"I am not fighting with God," said Stavro, fumbling with the words.

"I told you once before, Prometheus, and I will say it again — why do you find it so necessary to wrestle with every goat-

beard we meet? Stop smirking! I can name them for you . . .
Pappa Demetrios at Tigani, old Pappa Thoma, Father Eusebios,
and now this ill-fated old priest of Rogous. You tore their hearts
out with your questions. What are you trying to prove, that you
are smarter than they? Is this what Athens has done to you?"

"Are you finished?" said Stavro.

"No, I am not finished! I am sick and tired of this chip you
have on your shoulder. So, you lost a father and a brother . . .
but look at me, Prometheus — I lost a wife, two sons and,
begging your pardon, one daughter . . . I have more reason to
hate God than you . . ."

"Kapetan Thanasi is waiting for us," said Stavro. He could
feel his blood boiling inside him.

"Let him wait. I will tell you this for the last time, Prometheus — I do not like to see you ridiculing these people, daring
them to knock that chip off your shoulder. They are simple people . . . they get up in the morning, scratch the earth for a bite of
food, then crawl back to their huts. Do you think you can make
life easier for them with your wisdom and philosophy?"

Stavro turned and walked away from him. But in a thunderous voice, Petro yelled out, "A little learning has twisted your
head. You think you are clever, Prometheus, but you are foolish
. . . foolish!"

When Stavro caught up with the others, Kapetan Thanasi
looked at him austerely and said, "Is anything wrong with your
uncle?"

"No," said Stavro.

"He has not moved from that pile of ashes."

"He is thinking of the dead," Kleanthi exclaimed.

Kapetan Thanasi laughed. "And who of us does not think of
the dead? Stavro, go back . . . get him to move. We cannot expose ourselves here much longer."

"He does not listen to me," said Stavro.

Kapetan Thanasi lost his patience. "I cannot understand you
two," he cried. "Uncle and nephew, and you fight like dogs."

159

Stavro looked at the ground.

"From the first day he came to us," Kapetan Thanasi roared on, "you have buried yourself in resentment and hatred. I am not blind — he craves to talk to you. He is hungry for your love, but no, you spit in his face. What has he done for you to hate him so much?"

"I do not hate him," said Stavro, his head pounding.

"You *do* hate him — admit it!"

Angrily Stavro walked away. Kleanthi followed him, sticking close to his heels like a faithful dog. Still seething, Stavro touched him on the arm and said, "It will not be long, Kleanthi, before you return to your family. Perhaps you can go back to school — it is not too late. . . ."

"I will not see my father," said Kleanthi.

By this time Kapetan Thanasi had reached the highest point of aggravation with Petro. He glared back at him, motioned to him with both hands, shouted at him — but Petro would not move. Cursing out loud, Kapetan Thanasi went after him.

"It does not bother me any longer, Stavro . . . I mean, I can talk about my father and Pythagora without crying. . . ."

"It is best to forget everything," Stavro told him.

"You said you spoke with my father before . . . before you found him hanging from the plane tree. Tell me, what did he say to you, Stavro?"

"We talked about many things, Kleanthi."

"What were they?"

"This is not the time to bring them up."

"But I want to know. Why do you not tell me, Stavro?"

"Because they will upset you."

"I told you they do not bother me any longer . . . I told you!"

"Kleanthi, I do not want to fight with you."

"Then you will not tell me?"

"No."

The boy's face dropped. Feeling sorry for him, Stavro said, "Kleanthi, I loved your father. I shall never forget him, Kleanthi . . . no, never."

160

The boy turned his face away from Stavro. He tried to say something else but somehow the words did not come out. Stavro put his arm around him just as Kapetan Thanasi and Petro came beside them.

"Forward," cried Kapetan Thanasi, giving Kleanthi a firm push. Glaring fiercely at Stavro and Petro, he barked, "I do not want to hear another word from either of you until we get into Kalavryta . . . do I make myself clear?"

5

Kalavryta seemed like a stagnant lake of houses wedged in by towering mountains. It was much larger than Stavro had expected. As they moved into the city it did not appear that the war had touched the place . . . crowds walked freely in the streets, all the shops were open, children played gleefully in the schoolyard, and the coffeehouses had their awnings down as though it were still summer.

They stopped beside one of the shops while Kapetan Thanasi went inside to ask what time it was. When he came out he said, "How shall we do this? . . . I do not know where to begin."

"I saw a church back there," said Stavro. "Perhaps the priest knows about Pappa Lambro."

Petro pounced on him. "In the name of the Father, must we start looking for Pappa Lambro this very minute? I am tired and hungry!"

"Stavro is right," said Kapetan Thanasi. "The sooner we learn about your priest the better. Go, Stavro . . . we will wait for you here."

"Can we not wait in that coffeehouse?" said Petro. He pointed his finger across the street to a coffeehouse with a blue awning.

"Very well," said Kapetan Thanasi. "We will meet you there, Stavro."

"Can I go with him?" said Kleanthi.

"No," snapped Stavro.

The three crossed the street, leaving Stavro alone. He hurried toward the church but when he got there he discovered it was a chapel: the chapel of Saint Katerini. He found a young priest inside kneeling in front of the altar. He wore his robes and kalimafi. When he heard Stavro he stood up, startled. He was very tall and bony; his brown beard did not appear to be full-grown.

Stavro did not know how to ask him. He took a few steps toward the altar, then stopped.

"Yes," the priest said, "what is it . . . what do you want?"

"I did not mean to interrupt your prayer," Stavro replied.

"Speak . . . why are you here?"

In a shaking voice Stavro told him about Pappa Lambro, and after he had finished he could hear his heart pounding as though he dreaded to hear what the young priest might answer. But he looked at Stavro, unmoved. "I know nothing about your priest," he said coldly.

"Are you certain?"

"Would I not know if there was a strange priest in Kalavryta?"

Stavro felt his knees weakening. "Is there another church nearby?" he said.

"Who are you?" said the priest, eyeing him suspiciously. "I have not seen you before. . . ."

Stavro did not say another word to him. He walked to the door, opened it, and hurried out. In the street he asked a small boy where the church was; the boy pointed his finger down the street and told Stavro it was only a short walk away . . . he said it was a very large church, the Church of the Virgin, it had two great domes each with a clock. Stavro patted him on the head and continued on, passing more shops and coffeehouses. Across the street, the schoolhouse lay quiet now. The children had returned to their classrooms. Many faces walked past him, either very old or very young . . . toothless old men and women, emaciated children . . . they all smiled at Stavro and threw him

162

looks which if they could speak would say to him: *"Have mercy upon us . . . cleanse us . . . make us whole once again!"*

He came face to face with the church at exactly eleven-thirty. Both clocks showed the same time. He climbed up the front steps and opened the door. The church was empty. He hurried down the long marble aisle toward the altar. He heard voices from downstairs. From the top of the staircase in the altar he called out to them. He saw a head appear . . . a kalimafi, a long white beard. He heard the rustle of robes . . . the groaning voice of an old priest. "Who is it?"

He came and stood before Stavro, squinting hard into his face. "I do not know you," he said. "Where are you from?"

"Platano."

"Where is that?"

"In the south . . . near Kalamata."

"What brings you here?"

"I am looking for someone," said Stavro, again feeling his voice shake. "His name is Pappa Lambro. . . ."

"A priest?"

"Yes."

The old priest's face suddenly grew white. He fell back against the railing of the staircase and slumped weakly to his knees. Stavro helped him up but when his legs buckled again Stavro lifted him and carried him to a chair inside the altar. The old man's eyes were half-closed — his lips had turned purple. He mumbled something to Stavro . . . loose ends of words that Stavro could not piece together. The priest's breathing turned choppy and very labored — it seemed he was about to faint. Stavro slapped him on the cheeks, rubbed his wrists and hands. Slowly the color returned to his face. He let out a loud groan and pointed to the holy table. Stavro saw a bottle of wine there and went after it. He pulled out the cork and placed the neck of the bottle on the old man's lips. He took a quick drink, then crossed himself in fear.

"I was saving this for the liturgy," he blurted out. "May God

163

forgive me . . ." He brought up his eyes toward the Crucified Christ on the altar and held them there, terror-stricken. Stavro was afraid he might fall into a second fainting spell. He made him take another drink from the bottle. The agony was still imprinted on his face as he gasped out to Stavro, *"He is dead . . . your priest is dead!"*

"No!" cried Stavro. "No. . . ."

Slowly the old priest recovered his strength. He took one more sip from the bottle and stood up on wobbling feet. He walked to the Holy Table and placed the bottle on it. He looked at Christ as he spoke. ". . . He died many weeks ago. He was a skeleton — skin and bone. They forced him to work with a pick and shovel . . . a priest of God . . . a priest of God!"

"No," yelled Stavro. "I do not believe you!"

"He sleeps in our cemetery," the old priest went on, not listening to him. "If you wish I will show you the place."

"He is some other priest," Stavro cried out. "He is not Pappa Lambro. . . ."

"You are upset, my son — I can understand your pain."

"I tell you he is some other priest. Pappa Lambro still lives . . . he has to live!"

"I talked with him many times, my son . . . we cared for him in our hospital, but it was too late . . . we could not save him. I had forgotten but he did tell me his name was Lambro . . . that he came from a small village in the south, near Kalamata. . . ."

"Lambro is a common name . . . he could be someone else. He could be!"

"Did not your priest have a wife?"

"Yes."

"And was her name Eleni?"

"Yes."

"And did he also have a niece who came from Athens to live with him? I do not remember her name. . . ."

"Anna!" Stavro moaned. "Anna . . ." Unable to control himself any longer he burst into tears.

164

After a while he helped the priest with his coat and took hold of his arm. Together they walked out of the church into the street. The priest looked stronger now; he walked with swift steps and seemed very annoyed to have Stavro hold him by the arm.

They came to the cemetery.

The priest led Stavro through the squeaking iron gate and before going in himself, he made the sign of the cross three times. They proceeded for a short distance when suddenly the priest pointed to a mound of earth at the far end of the cemetery. It lay in the shadow of a tall cypress.

"There is your priest," he said.

A holy light hung over the grave. With mounting fear Stavro approached it. His hands shook as he struck a match. He could feel his body stiffen when he leaned over to ignite the holy light. After he lit it he stepped back, trembling. This could not be Pappa Lambro . . . this ugly bulge, this tumor, this heaving mound of earth swelling out its bowels as though it were gasping for a breath of air . . .

Again Stavro could not hold back his tears. The old priest took him in his arms and wept with him. "You did not know him," said Stavro, "and yet you weep."

"He was my brother in Christ . . . God's hand blessed us both."

Still looking at the grave, Stavro said, ". . . He baptized me . . . his hands joined my mother and father in marriage . . . he . . . he buried my brother, Stellio . . . He did all these things and I killed him. Yes, I killed him!"

But the old priest did not comprehend what Stavro was trying to say. He looked at Stavro sadly and replied, "I can understand how you must feel, my son — a priest is a right arm — you cannot lose it without suffering great anguish and pain. Look to God, He will sustain you."

"I cannot leave him here," said Stavro.

The priest looked at him, amazed.

165

"I must bring him back home with me," Stavro exclaimed.

"You speak foolishly, my son — Kalamata is more than one hundred kilometers from here."

"I have three friends — they will help me."

"And the Germans . . . have you forgotten the Germans?"

"Do you have a donkey?" Stavro asked him.

"Think twice, my son . . ."

"Do you have a donkey?"

"I do . . . I do."

"You must let me take it. I will return it, I promise."

The priest patted him fondly on the head. "I am an old man," he said. "A donkey cannot carry me where eventually I must go. Of course, you may have it; keep it as long as you wish. Now then, I would like to meet your friends. Where are they?"

"Waiting, in one of the coffeehouses," said Stavro.

"Come, there is nothing further you can do here. You have paid your respects to your priest."

Stavro gave one final look at the grave, then turned around and followed the old priest out of the cemetery. As they came into the street Stavro plunged himself into deep thought: *How could he face Anna . . . what would he say to her . . . ? And Pappa Lambro's wife, what about her . . . would he be able to find the words to explain to her, to ask her forgiveness . . . ?"*

The others were waiting impatiently under the blue awning of the coffeehouse. When Petro saw the priest, he yelled loud enough for Stavro to hear, "Kyrie eleison!"

Kapetan Thanasi rushed toward Stavro and grabbed hold of his arm. "Did you find your priest?" he cried.

Stavro looked directly into his uncle's eyes and said, "Pappa Lambro is dead. . . ."

Petro's mouth opened. "What did you say?" he cried.

"He is dead."

"No!"

"Yes," said the old priest, nodding his head mournfully. "He sleeps in our cemetery. . . ."

166

Petro eyed the priest up and down. "Who are you?" he snapped.

"I am Pappa Yerasimos . . . pastor of the Virgin's Church. I talked to your priest in his last moments . . . he had melted down to a shadow. God was merciful to take him out of his suffering. . . ."

"How do you know it was Pappa Lambro?" said Petro.

"Pappa Lambro talked to him," Stavro said. "He told him about Eleni . . . about Platano. . . ."

"In the name of the Father," Petro yelled, crossing himself. "You dragged us all this distance for nothing!"

Stavro felt his lips trembling. He saw Kleanthi looking at him, downcast. "It was foolish coming here," the boy exclaimed.

"That is not true!" Kapetan Thanasi yelled. "We were left with no other choice — we had to come."

Stavro's blood was boiling with guilt again. "Pappa Yerasimos is letting us have his donkey," he said.

Petro grimaced. "What do we want with a donkey?"

"I am going to take Pappa Lambro back with us."

"What?"

"I cannot leave him here," said Stavro.

"You mean, dig him out of the ground?" cried Petro.

"Yes."

"Kyrie eleison! Have you lost your senses, Prometheus? Hey, Pappa — speak to him. Tell him this is sacrilegious!"

The old priest cleared his throat. "There is nothing wrong with it," he said. "Since God enlightened the four of you to make this long journey, you cannot turn your faces on Him now and go back empty-handed. Alive or dead, your priest must return with you — it is God's will."

"Well-spoken, Pappa!" said Kapetan Thanasi. He slapped his thigh hard, then looked at Stavro. "Let us begin."

"Begin what?" Petro asked.

"The digging . . ."

Here Pappa Yerasimos flung up his hands. "No," he cried.

167

"There is no reason to hurry yourselves this way. Come to my house . . . eat and rest. Tomorrow, God willing, you can start back with your priest."

"You are a sensible man, Pappa," said Petro.

Stavro persisted. "Is it not better to get everything ready now and then rest tonight?"

"Prometheus, you have a hard head. You heard the priest — we do it tomorrow."

Kapetan Thanasi agreed. "It is best we make a fresh start tomorrow," he told Stavro.

Reluctantly Stavro nodded his head. "We must have Pappa Lambro out of the grave by dawn," he said.

"Stop worrying," Kapetan Thanasi replied. "We shall be well on our way by noon . . . I promise you."

It was still dark when Pappa Yerasimos got them out of bed the next day. Stavro was torn from a dream: he had been walking with Anna in the hills above Platano. It was autumn. Earth and sky sparkled in gold dust; behind them the sea heaved and sighed as though it had just awakened from a heavy sleep. They had not gone far when Anna turned suddenly around. She was holding a child in her arms and was offering it to Stavro. But he would not take it. Tears filled her eyes as she tried once more. In a fit of anger he brought up his hand and struck the child on the chest, knocking it out of Anna's arms and sending it against the rocks with a sickening thud. Before he could do or say anything he was awake and trembling in a cold sweat. He saw Pappa Yerasimos leaning over him, whispering into his ear, "Get up, my son . . . get up." He was holding a sheet of paper in his hand.

Stavro slid out of the bed. He took the paper and hurriedly glanced over it. "Where did you get this?" he asked.

"One of my parishioners brought it back from Corinth yesterday . . . he said the *'Little Birds'* dropped it from the sky. . . ."

"The *'Little Birds'*?"

"English planes! It was like a snowstorm, he told me . . . thousands fell . . . thousands!"

Kapetan Thanasi drew near them, rubbing his eyes. Petro and Kleanthi also heard the commotion.

"What is it?" Kapetan Thanasi was the first to speak. Stavro handed him the leaflet.

"English planes dropped this on Corinth yesterday," Stavro told him. Petro leaned over his shoulder.

"What does it say?" he asked.

"Yes, read it," Kleanthi cried out.

Stavro walked into the kitchen and stood over the jaki. He smoothed down the leaflet against his thigh, then brought it into the light of the flames. It was printed in bold letters and bore the strange title:

GENERAL EISENHOWER'S MESSAGE TO THE GREEK PEOPLE

ITALY HAS CRUMPLED. THE SOFT BELLY OF HITLER'S EUROPE NOW LIES EXPOSED. GREEKS, BE PATIENT A LITTLE LONGER. IN HER PERIL, GERMANY WILL STRIKE MORE SAVAGELY THAN EVER BEFORE. SHE WILL NOT HESITATE TO USE WEAPONS OF THE MOST ODIOUS BARBARISM, THE MOST DEVILISH DECEIT — HOPING TO DESTROY OR DISORGANIZE THE ACTIVE RESISTANCE OF THE GREEKS.

LET EACH MAN ABIDE BY THE INSTRUCTIONS OF HIS SUPERIORS.

LET THE VILLAGERS CONTINUE THEIR RESISTANCE.

LET THE PEASANT CONTINUE GIVING FOOD AND SHELTER TO THE NATIONAL GUERRILLA BANDS — AND LET HIM DENY FOOD TO THE ENEMY.

LET EVERY MAN DO HIS UTMOST TO HASTEN THE DESTRUCTION OF ALL ENEMY FORCES ON GREEK SOIL.

OUR WATCHWORD IS: UNITY AND DISCIPLINE!

GREEKS, BE ON YOUR GUARD . . . WE WILL INFORM YOU
WHEN THE HOUR STRIKES FOR GENERAL ACTION.

GENERAL DWIGHT D. EISENHOWER

Kapetan Thanasi closed his eyes for a moment. "God be
praised!" he cried.

"In the name of Christ," said Pappa Yerasimos, crossing himself, "our day of liberation is drawing near."

"If only Pappa Lambro were here to see this," Petro said.
He shook his head sadly and looked at Stavro.

"The coffee is ready," said the priest. "There is also bread
and a little cheese."

"We do not want to put you to any trouble," Stavro told him.

"Nonsense, my son — I only regret my wife is not here to
assist me in my last years. She died from a stroke . . . on the
very night the Italians invaded Greece."

"I am sorry to hear this," Kapetan Thanasi said.

Pappa Yerasimos sighed. "I should not complain . . . the
people here have been good to me. They bring me food, wash
my clothes, care for me when I am ill . . ."

"How many years do you have, Your Grace?" Kapetan Thanasi asked him.

"I am eighty-three. . . ." Pappa Yerasimos made a feeble effort to swell out his thin chest but was suddenly seized by a
coughing fit. Stavro brought him a glass of water. After a few
gulps the priest cleared his throat and said, "I have seen much
in my time . . . wars, internal strife, Turks, Italians, Germans,
one after another . . . I hope the day comes when we can
all breathe freely . . . when we can look at each other and
say: *Good morning, what a beautiful day it is!* The greatest evil
that arises from war is this — it deprives us of the simple things
. . . our awareness of the earth around us, the sea, the sky, a
dog, a goat . . . but above all our fellow man."

"I have never heard a better sermon, Pappa," Petro ex-

170

claimed. They all pulled up chairs and sat around the kitchen table. Before they could start eating, Kleanthi said to Stavro, "Who is Eisenhower?"

"He is an American general."

"What business do we have with him?"

"Little goat," Petro interrupted them, "do you not know that others are in this war beside ourselves? Do you think for one minute we can handle the Germans single-handed?"

"Why not?"

"Kyrie eleison! Open your eyes — many hands are helping us . . . British, American, French, Russian. . . ."

"Turks also?" said Kleanthi.

Petro laughed out loud.

"My father hated the Turks," Kleanthi went on. "He fought against them in the Balkans . . . he was in the Red Legion. . . ."

"I know," said Petro.

"Why?"

"Why what?" cried Petro.

"Why did he hate them so?"

"Little goat, it is a natural thing for a Greek to hate a Turk. Does not a cat hate a rat . . . and a sheep a mountain lion?"

"I have never seen a Turk. . . ."

"Pray God that day never comes, little goat."

"Does he have a black face, like an African?"

"Yes, and a black heart to go with it." Petro was about to say more but Stavro broke in, "Kleanthi, they have the same face as we."

"Close your mouth!" Petro yelled.

". . . We are alike in many ways, Kleanthi."

"Damn you, shut your mouth!" Petro bellowed. But Stavro paid no attention to him. He took hold of Kleanthi's arm and said, "Finish your breakfast — we have much work to do to-day."

Petro was seething, "You have now become a Turk-lover . . . a philosopher Turk-lover!"

171

Kapetan Thanasi tried to step between them but Petro shoved him off. He yanked Kleanthi away from Stavro and shouted into his face, "I will tell you about the Turk . . . I will tell you what he did to my great-grandmother's sister . . . !"

"There is no need for this!" Stavro yelled at him. But Petro was on fire, " . . . She had just given birth to her first child. . . ."

"Kleanthi, do not listen to him!"

"I am not afraid to hear it," the boy replied, twitching his face.

Petro gave Stavro an angry look before going on. "Little goat, you listen to me." he cried. "She was still very weak after having that first baby. That same day three Turks approached the house; they ambushed her husband while he was grazing his goats, slit open his throat and tossed him over a cliff. When the ill-fated woman heard his screams she came running out of the house clutching her baby. One of the Turks pulled the child out of her arms and with one stroke of his scimitar sliced the baby in two from head to groin. The two Turks then held the woman down while that same butcher defiled her. When he finished one of the other Turks climbed on her. They took turns . . . many turns. But it does not end here, little goat — those savages bit off her nipples and left her there like a dog on a street . . . !"

"Did she die?"

"She bled to death," Petro replied. "From two places she bled — her chewed-off breasts, and her . . ."

"Enough!" Stavro shouted, leaping to his feet. All this time Pappa Yerasimos kept nodding his head and not saying one word.

"Perhaps now, little goat, you will understand why a Greek hates a Turk," said Petro, wiping the sweat from his face with the back of his hand.

"I hate him too!" Kleanthi stammered.

"Of course . . . it is your sacred duty to hate him . . ." Petro did not have time to finish. Stavro grabbed him by the jacket and swung him around. He clenched his right fist — he had to fight with himself not to bring it up.

172

"Hit me," Petro cried. "I am your uncle . . . hit me!"

Stavro let him go. He saw Kapetan Thanasi glaring at him. Pappa Yerasimos placed his wrinkled hand on Stavro's shoulder and said, "You are highly excitable, my son — you must learn to control yourself."

"There was no need for him to say those things," Stavro fumed.

"You cannot hide the truth from the boy," said the priest. "He is bound to hear it one way or another."

"I thought we had learned to forget," said Stavro. "What good does it do, bringing these things up again and again . . . ?"

"I agree, my son. We are Christians and should love our neighbors, even though they are Turks. Here in Kalavryta the Turk lives with us, he eats and drinks with us, he goes to school with us. The past is over . . . done with; it must be forgotten once and for all. We are God's children — Turk as well as Greek. We work under one sun and sleep under the same stars."

Stavro looked at Kleanthi — the boy's face was white. He had stopped eating and was playing with a piece of dark bread, picking it up and laying it down over the same spot on the table.

"Eat!" Stavro yelled at him.

"I am not hungry."

"You must nourish yourself, my son," said Pappa Yerasimos. "You have a hard day before you."

"Do I have to come to the cemetery with you?"

"Yes," said Kapetan Thanasi.

"I do not like to look at death."

"You are coming . . . not another word!"

The priest got up. "I too shall join you," he said. He crossed himself slowly and uttered a soft prayer. Stavro waited for him to finish, feeling very uneasy. They all followed the priest outside. He went around the house and into a small shed. He came out holding a shovel in his hands. He gave it to Stavro.

"Forward, my children," he said to all of them. He lifted his fingers and blessed them. "Do your cross . . . ask God to give you strength and courage for this day."

173

They followed him into the yard. Petro had a long face and was not talking; Kleanthi stuck close to Stavro. Kapetan Thanasi took hold of the priest's arm and walked side by side with him.

The morning was still gray and dark. The last sounds of night had died down save for a crowing rooster in a nearby yard. When they passed the church, Pappa Yerasimos did his cross. Turning sharply around, he made certain Kleanthi did likewise. He did not seem to concern himself with the others.

Inside the cemetery the priest stopped to squint at the graves. Although Stavro remembered where Pappa Lambro lay, he waited for the old priest to point out the place. Quickly they formed a circle around the grave and stood there looking at it silently. Suddenly Petro burst into tears. He slid to his knees and kissed the mound of earth, moaning and sobbing. Kapetan Thanasi had to pull him away. Petro got very angry.

"Leave me alone," he cried. "I want to mourn for my priest."

Stavro began digging. With every spadeful of earth that was tossed up Pappa Yerasimos leaned over to touch it with his fingers and bless it, saying, "In the name of the Father, and the Son, and the Holy Ghost. Amen . . ."

After a while Stavro stopped to wipe the sweat from his face. Kapetan Thanasi took the shovel away from him and started jabbing it into the ground. Petro stood red-eyed beside the priest, and behind him, Kleanthi.

It did not take Kapetan Thanasi long to reach the casket — a pine box with painted black crosses still legible on both sides and top. Stavro took hold of one end, Kapetan Thanasi the other, but they could not lift it. Kapetan Thanasi motioned to the others with his eyes. Petro came into the hole and stood beside Kapetan Thanasi — Kleanthi helped Stavro. They dislodged the casket from its hold on the earth and lifted it, easing it carefully over the side until it rested on two small mounds of loose earth. Only then did Stavro see the boots all around him . . . German boots!

174

Instantly his mind went to his revolver, but when he saw more German soldiers swarming into the cemetery, surrounding them from all sides, he shuddered. They planted themselves six feet apart, their automatic rifles drawn and pointed at the grave.

With one final, hopeless look toward the casket Stavro waited for them to come.

6

At daybreak the church bells began ringing. From inside the schoolhouse where the Germans had taken them, Stavro could hear the town crier shouting in the street:

"The Germans order all inhabitants of Kalavryta to assemble in the schoolhouse . . . men, women, and children. He who refuses to come will be executed!"

He went to the window and saw German soldiers breaking into the shops and coming out with their arms full, confiscating whatever they could find. While this was going on other soldiers entered the houses in groups of three and dragged out the young girls. Their screams pierced Stavro's eardrums.

By mid-morning the schoolhouse was crammed. There was not enough room to turn around or move an arm. Children clutched their mothers' hands; old women shook their heads and moaned in death-heavy sounds. Many fainted.

Stavro looked everywhere but he could not locate Pappa Yerasimos. He turned to Kapetan Thanasi, who was standing at his side, and said to him, "Where is the priest?"

"They released him," Kapetan Thanasi replied.

"Are you certain?"

"I heard them with my own ears — they said, *'Let him go . . . he is too old.'* "

Stavro kept one eye on his uncle. Petro was crouched low beside the window, studying his hands, not saying one word.

175

"Are you all right?" Stavro asked him.

Petro snorted. "As if you care what happens to me!"

Stavro offered him his hand. "Uncle Petro," he mumbled, "I am sorry for what I said to you. . . ."

Again Petro snorted.

". . . I do not know what comes over me. . . ."

"I will tell you what comes over you," Petro exclaimed. "This whole idea of yours was insane. I knew we would never find Pappa Lambro alive . . . I knew it! But no, you had to keep at it . . . forcing us to come to this ill-fated place. Well, I hope you are satisfied. You shit in your pants to get us here, and now we will never leave alive."

"Please take my hand, Uncle Petro. . . ."

"Why should I?"

"I am asking your forgiveness."

"You should ask God to forgive you — not me!"

"I do not care about God's forgiveness. I want only yours."

Petro looked at him disgustedly. "You need them both, Prometheus . . . both!" he cried.

Just as Stavro started to lower his hand Petro reached out and took it. "Prometheus," he grinned, "no other nephew in all the world would treat his uncle as you treat me . . . but I must love you very much." His eyes clouded. He swept Stavro into his arms and embraced him. "You are my brother's son," he said. "Perhaps some day you will realize how much I truly love you. . . ."

Stavro was choked with tears — he could not speak. Petro pushed him away for a moment and measured him suspiciously. "Why do you ask my forgiveness?" he said. "Is it because you too believe that everything is hopeless for us?"

"That is not so," said Stavro.

"We shall not come out of this . . . not one living soul."

Kapetan Thanasi and Kleanthi made their way through the terror-stricken faces and finally came beside them. Kapetan Thanasi said, "Are you both all right?"

176

Petro scowled. "Friend Kapetan," he said, "I have strong convictions about this sort of thing . . . as I told you many months ago — life is a scale. Thus far we have been fortunate indeed . . . it has tilted in our favor. But as of this moment, friend Kapetan, the German has his thumb on it."

"Do not lose heart," Kapetan Thanasi told him.

"Are they going to kill us?" said Kleanthi. He was looking only at Stavro; the boy's face was drained of color.

"They only intend to frighten us," Stavro answered in a hoarse voice.

"They have done that," Petro exclaimed. "They have frightened the shit out of me!"

"There are too many women and children among us," Kapetan Thanasi interjected. "This is one thing the German has never done . . . he has not laid a finger on a woman or a child. . . ."

"We are dreamers," Petro cried. "Dreamers . . . !"

Stavro saw a trace of tears in Kleanthi's eyes. He touched the boy on the shoulder and said, "Kleanthi, listen to me — I am certain the Germans will not harm us. They might keep us here for the rest of the day, without food or water . . . but they will not harm us."

"Tell him the truth!" Petro screamed at him.

"It is the truth."

"They are going to kill us, little goat . . . mark my words, they are going to kill us!"

Kleanthi started to cry. Petro blocked his ears and turned his face toward the window. Just then the door opened; German soldiers shoved their way into the crowded rooms. They opened a narrow aisle for an officer to pass through — a thin tight-lipped major with black-rimmed glasses and a stark white face. When he reached the front of the room he turned and faced everyone.

"I want all the men and boys to walk slowly outside . . ." he snapped. But no one moved. Again he barked out the order. The soldiers all around him lifted their automatic rifles in one motion. Screams and moans filled the schoolhouse. One by one the men and boys filed through the crowd and out the door. More soldiers were waiting for them in the schoolyard, their rifles up. Stavro and his uncle were among the last to leave. As soon as they stepped outside two soldiers slammed the door shut and stood guard beside it.

"In the name of the Father," Petro groaned, "what do they intend to do with those ill-fated women and children?"

Stavro did not have time to answer him. The soldiers began prodding them with the butt ends of their rifles, forcing them into lines, three abreast. The lines extended all the way across the schoolyard and into the street. At a command from the thin major they started marching out of the yard, guarded on both sides by scores of soldiers each screaming at them in frenzied voices and commanding them to move faster.

Pappa Yerasimos suddenly appeared.

With futile strides he tried to keep up with the marching lines. "Courage, my children," he shouted at them. "God is great . . . He will save us . . . courage!"

A German soldier beside the priest let him rant on. Petro turned his head and whispered to Stavro, "Do you have your revolver?"

"No," said Stavro. "They took it."

"Kapetan Thanasi's also?"

"Yes."

Petro looked around him, confused. "Where are they taking us?" he cried.

"I do not know," said Stavro.

"Today, I shall be in paradise with my wife and children . . ." Petro suddenly exclaimed.

"Do not talk that way!" Stavro yelled at him.

" . . . Yes, I can see my brother there, waiting for me with his arms open . . . I see Stellio too . . . and also Pappa Lambro. . . ."

178

"Uncle Petro — please stop."

"Prometheus, I know about the girl . . . Kapetan Thanasi told me everything!"

They moved across the street, past the bank and up a long slope leading to the white stucco gymnasion. At the top of the slope they stopped. Someone let out a piercing cry; every Greek head snapped suddenly around.

The school was in flames!

A few men broke away from the lines and started running down the slope, screaming. A quick volley from the automatic rifles brought them all down. Petro's hand found Stavro's — it was cold and soaked with sweat. A dozen meters in front of them Stavro saw Kleanthi fall to his knees sobbing. One of the Greeks at his side went to pick him up but a German soldier darted in between them and struck the boy a glancing blow on the head with the butt of his rifle. Dazed, Kleanthi lay there on the ground. The German soldier tugged him to his feet and made him walk.

"You bastards," Petro shouted out loud. "You dirty white-blooded bastards!"

But in the turmoil no one heard him.

They continued past the slope and up another small hill not far from the cemetery. The thin major ordered everyone to stop. He climbed a large boulder and after they had all quieted down, he shouted, "Greeks of Kalavryta, we brought you up here so that you can see how beautifully your city burns . . ." The soldiers planted their feet wide apart and started laughing almost hysterically. The major silenced them and went on: "We have counted carefully . . . there are over eight hundred of you here . . . and almost two thousand in that schoolhouse . . . you can thank those guerrilla butchers at Kerpini for what is about to happen to you!"

Stavro's heart fell when he saw the major point his finger toward the base of a sharp cliff. He then ordered the soldiers to back everyone against it. Four machine guns were brought out

179

and placed twenty meters from each other. Several soldiers bent over the guns and started feeding them long belts of cartridges.

Stavro kept looking at Kleanthi — the boy could not stop crying. His body shook so badly Stavro was afraid he would fall to the ground in a fit. One of the soldiers noticed this and yanked Kleanthi into the front line between two old men whose frozen eyes were fixed on the machine guns. Kapetan Thanasi was standing directly behind them.

Petro was now speechless. He had a firm grip on Stavro's hand and kept squeezing it with all his strength. In a moment of terror he slid around Stavro and hid behind him, still holding his hand. Hot lumps of agony swelled inside Stavro's heart . . . but it was Anna who frightened him and not the four machine guns . . . Anna, forced to live out the rest of her life alone . . . haunted by the presence of his child . . . *his child!* Her words suddenly struck him like the clang of a bell: *"You must keep on looking for God, Stavro . . . you must!"* She will never know how much he *did* look for Him . . . how many times he fell on his knees before Him, this ghost of a God, this deaf-mute, this elusive shadow. But no, He was not to be found . . . He is a fraud, this God — a deceitful hypocrite of a fraud!

Both Kleanthi and Kapetan Thanasi fell with the first blast from the machine guns. Stavro felt his uncle's hands on his back, knocking him to the ground. He heard bullets splattering into flesh behind him, into pain . . . into death. Now the full weight of Petro's body was upon him — his uncle's arms encircling him, protecting him, absorbing still another burst of bullets.

"Prometheus — I . . . I am not afraid," the harsh gasping words thundered inside Stavro's ears. He dared not move — even after Petro's warm blood fell soothingly over his face as though it too were reaching out to protect him.

The final torment flowed from Petro's mouth. "I have always loved you, Stavro . . . do me this last favor. If . . . if he is a boy . . . name him. Name him . . . !"

180

Stavro feigned death when the German boots approached him. They kicked Petro away; kicked Stavro in the mouth, in the stomach, in the groin. But he did not make a sound. Slowly the boots moved off. Inside his pounding ears Stavro heard more angry kicks, more insane laughter . . . and now the sharp stings of revolvers — endlessly, endlessly. There was a long silence and then he heard singing . . . *German voices marching away, singing!* By this time his uncle's blood had dried on his face. It started to itch but he dared not move or breathe or open his eyes.

Something touched his head. He felt a warm hand on his face. Slowly, fearfully he opened his eyes and saw Pappa Yerasimos bending over him. Stavro let out a tortured cry and fell into the priest's arms, sobbing.

7

At dawn the next day he had Pappa Lambro out of the casket and in a strong burlap sack. Instead of his donkey Pappa Yerasimos managed to get two mules. He helped Stavro lift Pappa Lambro and sling him over the mule that was already carrying Kleanthi. Kapetan Thanasi and Petro were tied down to the other mule.

After Stavro had tied Pappa Lambro securely he laced both mules together with one rope and led them out of the cemetery into the street. Pappa Yerasimos was only one step behind him.

"Your journey will be a safe one, my son," he said. "The Germans have already moved north . . . to Athens."

Only a few houses and shops remained standing; also the church. Everything else was smoldering in ashes. The hands of one clock on the church were not moving — they still said two-thirty. Pappa Yerasimos could not take his eyes away from them.

"That evil hour will never leave us," he said in a suffering voice. "It is our acropolis, our sacred temple. Let the world come here and see what cruel things man can do to himself when he has abandoned God. . . ."

"I shall bring back the mules," Stavro said to him.

"In time, my son — in time."

"I promise to take good care of them."

Pappa Yerasimos smiled. "When you bury your priest," he said, "and your uncle also, and your two friends — give them a final kiss for me." The old priest then extended his hand for Stavro to kiss. Stavro drew back. But then he thought of Pappa Lambro . . . he thought of Pappa Demetrios at Tigani, Father Eusebios, the monks at the Monastery of the Great Cave . . . he thought of his uncle's blood that had already found its way through Stavro's pores to join his own blood . . . he thought of Kapetan Thanasi and Kleanthi . . . of Pythagora and Pelopida . . . even that dead German boy lying in the snow near Potami . . . and suddenly the torment of his guilt was too much to bear.

The old priest's wrinkled hand again invited him. With tears streaking down his face Stavro seized it and kissed it. Pappa Yerasimos touched him with his fingers and blessed him. "Go to the Good, my son," he said. "May God protect you always. . . ."

They embraced for the last time. Stavro gave a firm pull on the rope. Slowly the mules trudged down the street. Not one child came out to tease them or dash around them or pull their tails. Sorrow, like the heavy pall of black clouds overhead, lay heavy in every corner of the city. Even the death-laden mules seemed anxious to leave Kalavryta and lose themselves in the hills.

Once there, Stavro did not look back.